The Night Bell

Megan Weiler

The Night Bell

PICADOR

First published 2001 by Picador
an imprint of Macmillan Publishers Ltd
25 Eccleston Place, London SW1W 9NF
Basingstoke and Oxford
Associated companies throughout the world
www.macmillan.com

ISBN 0 330 48264 5

1 3 5 7 9 8 6 4 2

A CIP catalogue record for this book is available from
the British Library.

Typeset by Intype London Ltd
Printed and bound in Great Britain by
Mackays of Chatham plc, Chatham, Kent

for Bill

I ONCE DREAMT that I was attending some public spectacle and I suddenly saw my father in the crowd. I hadn't seen him for a long time. He looked completely transformed: twenty, thirty years younger, the way I knew from photographs that he had once looked. His face had lost its bags and wrinkles; it was smooth and compact. His nose was no longer swollen; his eyes were clear; his figure was as slender as in his youth, and he had once again drawn the belt of his trousers tightly, to show off his small waist.

'Christof!' I exclaimed.

I had an impulse to embrace him, but I held back. Something told me that now he did not want to be embraced. There was a marked, almost statuesque coolness in his manner, as if his handsome features, his strong profile and clear complexion had been chiselled in marble. He seemed to be aware only of himself, of his own miraculous achievement. I realized that in order to look like this he must have slept for days and weeks and months, barely eating or drinking, just deeply resting, unburdening himself bit by bit of his life: dreaming it all away along with the outward signs of age and degradation.

He was proud, but he was not happy. No one could know

what he had gone through to turn the clock back like that, passing through that zone of death. He had no time for my amazement, my joy of recognition. He was impatient with me, I could tell. It was my mother he wanted to see. Or rather, it was she by whom he wanted to be seen. He wanted to show himself to her in triumph.

Later in the dream, I saw my mother sitting on my father's lap. They were flirting and playing with each other like a very young couple, practically still children.

Part One

I

ON THE AEROPLANE I suddenly felt a terrible misgiving, it was almost like a physical giving-way. I thought about getting out, pulling the emergency brake – but this was not a train. I was trapped, thousands of feet above the ocean, on my way to Zurich. I sat pressed against my seat, overwhelmed by the thought that I was flying *in the wrong direction*.

During the remainder of the flight I was unable to make myself think about arriving. Instead I thought about the fat girl sitting next to me. I had worried that whoever sat next to me would want to talk to me; but once silence was established between us, I became intensely curious about this girl. She was reading *The Old Man and the Sea* translated into French. I tried to engage her in conversation when our dinner was served, but she was not forthcoming, and I learned only that she lived in Atlanta and was going to Paris for a week.

The arrivals hall in Zurich was divided by a pane of glass, with friends and families of arriving passengers pressed up against the outside, forming a solid wall of faces. Although I had landed here many times before, I had forgotten this aspect of the airport and it gave me a slight shock. I did not see my father among the faces at the glass. I didn't want to appear to be anxiously searching, in case he was not there; or in case, even though I couldn't see him, he was there and saw me. I looked again casually, letting my eyes roam leisurely across the crowd with a mildly smiling expression. I wanted to convey indifferent contemplation with perhaps a touch of irony, amusement at the sight of all these people eagerly expectant. He was not there. I secured a luggage cart and stood by the moving conveyor belt, my back turned to the glass, waiting for my suitcase. No problem. I would call to make sure he wasn't on his way, and then I would simply take the train. I would have preferred all along to take the train. In fact I had tried to dissuade my father from coming to pick me up, I had almost begged him not to. It was only when he said that Silke was coming with him that I had given in.

I should have been relieved, but a feeling of panic was churning in my stomach. I wondered if it was merely from uncertainty, or if it was the fear of meeting him, suppressed during the trip, that was being released now that he didn't seem to be here. My suitcase appeared almost immediately. For once I would have wished it to have taken longer. I wheeled the cart very slowly toward the exit. There was an exchange window, and I hesitated in front of it, debating whether to buy enough Swiss francs for the train ride or just enough for a phone call. There was not a single customs person to ask me questions or search through my luggage. Before I knew it I was on the outside. And there, in the midst of the crowd, stood my father, all by himself.

The moment of first seeing my father always overwhelms me.

When I try to summon that moment now, I picture him lighting a cigarette, concentrating intently on the flame. But I don't believe he actually had a cigarette. There must have been something else, in his pose or expression, to suggest that air of complete absorption. He was simply standing there, I think, looking down at the floor. Despite the many people milling about, my father seemed to be standing in a space of his own, a clearing, as if a certain radius around him remained empty. The odd thing was that he didn't seem to be looking for me.

He didn't see me as I approached him. He looked bad: his skin was greyish and there were large bags under his eyes. But he was smartly dressed, wearing his black beret and a navy trenchcoat and – I noticed these particularly – sumptuous new trousers made of white, thick-waled corduroy. For a second I stared incredulously at the trousers. He still hadn't seen me.

I had to raise my voice above the din: 'Christof!'

We embraced. I kissed him, or rather placed my head alongside his and then instinctively withdrew, while he was still moving to kiss me on the other side.

As we walked through the airport toward the car park, he told me about the difficulties he had had getting there on time. There had been a terrible traffic jam on the highway. The car parks had been filled; there had been signs guiding him from building A to B to C and so forth, until finally he had found a spot in building G, quite a distance away. And then the flight number I had given him in my letter was not announced anywhere. He had rushed here and there asking people, until finally someone had suggested that he wait in the spot where I had found him.

'Shall we first have a cup of coffee?' he asked suddenly. 'Before we drive home?'

'Sure, that's fine with me.'

I thought that he might need coffee to drive. We were standing in line at a window to pay for the car park and I suddenly thought I saw the ticket in his hand shaking. I looked again; but now he was holding both hands together, with the ticket, and they were perfectly still. I remembered that he had always prided himself on the steadiness of his hand in the laboratory, injecting mice or pipetting. He had shown me how difficult it was to hold my hand perfectly still for a prolonged time, without wavering or trembling. He could do it better than most people.

I felt certain that he had caught me looking at his hand and had steadied it by an effort of will.

'Shall we? Or would that make everything too complicated?' He got out of the queue, unable to make up his mind; then decided to pay after all and stood again at the back of the line.

'Let's just get on the road,' he said. 'We can always go to a rest stop along the way.'

'Good idea,' I answered, aiming for a light-hearted tone in order to reassure us both.

Climbing into the passenger seat of his little Fiat, I was all at once surrounded by a familiar mix of tobacco and other aromas. It seemed to come from the distant past, from my childhood. Although he had bought this car after I had left for America, its dusty interior felt like a place which, a long time ago, had been my home. The smell was protective, comforting, telling me everything would be all right. I suddenly felt an intense happiness, as if I had only now recognized my father.

* * *

A few months earlier, I had received a letter from him in which he mentioned that he was about to retire. My father's tone was sanguine. Thanks to a favour owed him, he wrote (with typical, unnecessary frankness), his grant had been extended for another year, so that he would be able to continue his research even after he was officially retired.

The letter was accompanied by a clipping from the university newspaper describing the scientific convention that had been held in my father's honour. Former students and colleagues had gathered, some of them having travelled all the way from America. The writer of the article said that my father was an 'intellectual role model', who still 'radiated' enthusiasm for his subject. The president of the university had said in his speech that my father was noted for his 'humaneness'.

My father was quoted as saying, 'Now I will have to find a new hobby.'

I knew that his use of the word *hobby* was carefully weighed, intentional; the point was that science had been play for him. At this unique opportunity for self-definition, he was suggesting the privilege of genius, for whom work and play are one and the same thing.

Still, I was sure his comment had endeared him to the audience. Here it was, his farewell from his profession, in which, despite the eulogies, he had not gone as far as had been expected. Doubtless many were looking at their own lives' work, wondering how it would appear when all summed up, glad they still had some years to go. And yet he was saying cheerfully, 'Don't feel sorry for me. I'm all right. I'm only giving up one hobby and I'll find another.'

What aplomb! He walks on water!

Accompanying the article was a blurry black-and-white photo of my father, apparently taken while he had been listening to one of the lectures. The photograph jarred painfully with both the article and my father's letter. He looked dishevelled, lost and anxious, as though unable to comprehend the proceedings. He looked like someone attending his own funeral.

When I saw this picture, I felt shaken. Paradoxically, it was as though I had just received word that my father was not dead yet. I had given him up for dead: but he was still alive.

I had booked my flight that same week.

2

I DREAM THAT my parents are separating again. It's a strange thing to dream since they have been divorced now for over twelve years. Nor have I forgotten this in my dream: it is not a regressive dream, not a dream about twelve years ago. Rather, its premise is that they were reunited, perhaps only very briefly, for the flash of an idea; and now the whole long process of separation must be started all over again.

This is the proportion: their being together is like no time at all compared to the never-ending process of separation.

The separation that is going on in my dream consists in my mother cleaning out a room full of old stuff, sorting through it, looking at each object individually and deciding whether or not to keep it. Sometimes she holds up something that belonged to my brother or me, a toy or an old pair of ice-skates. She asks if we want them. The remarkable thing is that I know, and my mother knows, that once she has emptied out this room completely she and my father are going to get back together again for a brief period. She is hurrying to the room before this happens, so that afterwards she can resume the job of separation by starting with another room.

There is no end to the rooms.

*

I have often heard the story of how they met. My mother was a graduate student in neurophysiology at Stanford. She studied the brains of fish. My father, a postdoc from Germany, worked in a different laboratory, so they knew each other only from afar. In order to strike up a closer acquaintance, my father said to my mother one day, 'I've just read a good book that has to do with fish,' and he lent it to her. The book was *Five Red Herrings* by Dorothy Sayers, a murder mystery.

That is the first part of the story I've been told.

The second part comes later, after an interval of uncertain length. They were walking on the beach together, and my father said: 'You know, I think I'd like to keep you.' My mother asked: 'For how long?' He replied, 'Oh, for ever.'

I've always thought that I couldn't imagine a nicer proposal, perhaps because my mother sounded so happy in the way she recounted it to me.

After my parents separated, I began to call my father by his first name, Christof, in order to put a distance between us. I felt this was a relief to him, too: it seemed to relieve him of a burden. It was a relief to us both. So effective has it been that when I think of his name, 'Christof', it only summons up a vague notion, as of a person I barely know.

But if I say the name by which I used to call him, *Papi*, it causes a little shock in me, like an electric current stirring in the depths of memory. Because I haven't used it for so long it is still filled with his presence, his voice, his smell, all the things I find it impossible to summon up by force of will. It contains his essence, that same essence that took me by surprise when I climbed into his little Fiat in the airport car park.

*

As we were leaving the car park, another car was waiting for my father's spot. The pressure of this unnerved him and he stalled the motor in backing out. We had to descend from the top floor of the building. My father hesitated at each level, uncertain whether to turn left or right, although the ramp spiralled always in the same direction. As I played the guide, reading street signs in the traffic maze surrounding the airport, I suddenly realized that my father had been more afraid of our meeting than I.

'I should tell you that Großmutti was in the hospital,' he said when we were on the road. 'She had an intestinal problem, and it was quite bad for a while. But she's out again, and seems to be getting better. I just talked to Erika yesterday. – Großmutti is looking forward to your visit,' he added.

I was silent for a moment. Although I knew he didn't mean it this way, I felt his telling me immediately about my grandmother as a reproach, as if I hadn't been thinking about her enough. At the same time, an intestinal problem sounded less serious than my grandmother's mental decline, which I understood had been drastic in the three years since I'd last seen her. In a recent letter, my aunt Erika had told me that she no longer recognized the names of my cousins.

'Does she even remember who I am?' I blurted out, as if catching my father in a lie.

'Oh yes, she knows who you are. I've been telling her every time I talk to her that you are coming to visit her soon.'

I couldn't think of anything to say. I felt slightly ashamed.

Our road left the industrial environs of Zurich behind and cut through the countryside. It was late April and everything was intensely green. I looked out at the juicy cow pastures and the blossoming apple and pear orchards. I silently celebrated the joy I always felt in returning to this landscape in which I had grown up. We drove through small towns: Winterthur, Frauenfeld, Romanshorn. I was amazed at the half-timber houses, the red geraniums spilling out of window boxes, the old-fashioned tavern signs, at the solid and heavy, well-fed, neatly groomed appearance of everything. America as I knew it was a more tattered place; the cities were dirty, unruly and dangerous; even in the nicest neighbourhoods the houses were built out of flimsy wood from which the paint was always peeling off. America suited me, it suited the person I'd become; but still a feeling of nostalgia overcame me as I took in these forgotten sights.

We stopped at a petrol station. My father went into the building to pay. I noticed it was also a bar and restaurant. He did not come out for a long time, and I guessed that he was having a drink.

When we were on the road again he asked me about my mother: 'How is she? I mean, how is she *really*?'

His voice sounded somehow fearful, as if he scarcely dared to ask.

'Fine,' I said. I told him about a scientific paper she had just published.

'Has she changed much?' he persisted. 'Does she have grey hair? I haven't even seen a picture of her in years.'

I felt torn. After all, they were married for over twenty years, so perhaps he did deserve some kind of answer. 'Yes, of course, she's aged a little, yes, she has some grey hair.' But that's all I would say, that's where I drew the curtain.

'I can't even picture her any more.'

*

There was no one at home when we arrived at the house. Silke was still in the laboratory and her children, Stefan and Brigitte, were at school. My father called Silke on the phone. 'She won't be back for another hour,' he said to me, cupping his hand over the receiver. 'Shall I make us a frozen pizza for lunch?'

'Sure!'

'Irene wants pizza!' he shouted into the receiver, as if I had demanded it. 'And then she wants to sleep.'

While the pizza was in the oven, he didn't know what to do with me. 'Just make yourself comfortable,' he said. 'You know which one is your room downstairs.'

I remembered the first time I had stayed in Silke's house, shortly after my father had moved in. I had found a vase of flowers in the room and chocolates on the pillow. I was surprised by the power of these things to console me – as if no hurt in me could be so great that it couldn't be soothed away by a little beauty and luxury. Perhaps I had been so filled with fear and resistance that I had simply longed for some other emotion. It was the anonymity of this welcome that cheered me more than anything. I didn't have to connect the flowers and chocolates with Silke: they had placed themselves there of their own accord to greet me.

I put down my luggage and looked around. The bed was made with crisp white embroidered sheets and huge German pillows. This time Silke had put a bottle of mineral water and a glass on the desk for me, along with several little plates filled with fruits and crackers in case I was hungry.

I washed my face and began to put some of my clothes into the closet. I never had trouble making myself at home in a strange house. It occurred to me that the people in whose houses I stayed would be shocked to know how easy it was for me.

3

My earliest memories of my father are the two heavy sweaters that he used to wear all the time. He wore them for many years, throughout most of my childhood. One was a Norwegian fisherman's sweater, a sort of dirty white in colour with a pattern of black spots. The other sweater was light blue and had been knitted by my grandmother. Although it seemed a quite ordinary light blue colour, I have never seen a colour like it anywhere else: so opaque and dense, unlike the sky or water, the colour earth would be if it were blue.

And of course his pipe – he was never without it. There is an old home movie in which my father, wearing the Norwegian sweater, with a brightly coloured tam-o'-shanter on his head, a scarf around his neck, and his pipe clenched between his teeth, is building a snowman with my help in front of our little rented brick house in Glenside, Pennsylvania. I am not much help since I am very small, but I do my best, rolling the ball of snow around in the garden until it grows so big that I have to lean against it with all my weight to make it budge.

How jauntily he wears that cap! There is a stage-presence about him, a sense of irony, as if he had purposefully planted certain slight incongruities, such as the exaggerated angle of the tam, or the pipe (which cannot possibly be lit), in order that it should be impossible simply to take him at face value, a father making a snowman with his little daughter in front of his suburban house. He is thoroughly enjoying himself, he loves seeing his child tumble about: but nonetheless he is playing a role.

He is about thirty-five years old and medium height, just under six foot, with brown hair and light blue eyes. He is a researcher, a biologist. He is German and speaks English with a British accent because of a year spent in London before coming to America. He is going to be famous, it's only a matter of time before he makes a great discovery. And even that will be done playfully, effortlessly or rather with mock effort, the way he helps me to roll my ball of snow. We give the snowman a cap, a scarf, and a pipe, too.

I remember my father taking me to school in first grade. As he let me out of the car he used to say, '*Gute Nacht, schlaf gut*,' as if he were confused and thought he was tucking me into bed. The joke seemed fresh each time, as I delightedly protested and corrected him.

*

Our early home movies show walks in the woods in Pennipack Park; my serious round face set aglow by the birthday candles I am about to blow out; Easter, with me toddling around the grass finding treasure after treasure hidden in clumps of crocuses or behind the daffodils; Halloween and Christmas. I've watched these scenes so often they seem like memories: the whole year a series of wonderful surprises. It is my mother who creates these surprises, invents all the many rituals by which we live. My mother, Helen, grew up on a farm in sunny

California. She has light, loosely curled hair and wears pretty home-made dresses with small waists and wide skirts; when the camera is on her she is always busy, bustling, as if she couldn't spare it a moment. This is from shyness and an attempt to appear natural. Both of my parents, filming each other, are flirtatious, with bright expressions.

I am four when my brother Martin comes along; now he is already one year old, beaming at my mother with a face like a little golden bun fresh out of the oven.

One summer day, a big black splendid rabbit turned up in our back yard. He was tame. The people from whom he had run away said we could keep him. His name was Charcoal. He lived henceforth on our back porch and we fed him lettuce and carrots and dandelion leaves.

I remember the heavy, warm rabbit smell of Charcoal when I put my arms around him.

*

When I was seven my father received an invitation to join the faculty of a newly founded university in a beautiful town on a lake in Southern Germany. My parents discussed it. My mother would have preferred to stay in America, but for my father it was a dream come true: to be able to return to his home country as a full, tenured professor.

His new university paid for all of us to travel as first-class passengers on the ship *Europa*, sailing from New York to Bremerhaven. Crossing the Atlantic in first class was one of the last true luxuries, my father would say later, after passenger liners had stopped crossing the Atlantic. The inference was clear that the first class of these noble vessels was different from that of aeroplanes the way an aristocrat differed from a boorish nouveau riche. The fact that his university paid for our trip made my father feel, I think, that the rest of his life from now on was going to be first class, the aristocratic kind.

On this trip I kept my first diary. In it I recorded, in a childishly clumsy handwriting and with many misspellings, events such as the sighting of dolphins or seagulls; or the fact that I went with my mother to drink coffee in one of the ship's lounges and the band was playing.

But what I actually remember from the voyage is something completely different from dolphin sightings or listening to the band.

On the first evening after our departure, the captain gave a state dinner and dance to welcome the first-class passengers. A steward brought dinner trays for my brother and me; we had a separate cabin adjoining my parents'. While we ate, my parents were getting dressed up in their evening finery. Then they left, kissing us goodnight.

Martin and I lay on the beds in the unfamiliar room. It was still too early to go to sleep, and I remember the room being very brightly lit, the white sheets reflecting the lamplight. We played with the toys we had brought. I was happy about a new little doll that I had, with pliable limbs and a pink dress. We both, at about the same time, began to feel sick. We felt sicker and sicker, and started rolling around on the beds in discomfort. There was no way to reach my mother. She had gone off who knows where in that enormous labyrinthine ship, dressed in a silk blouse and long skirt. I was convinced that our food had been poisoned and we had been left to die, our cries and moans unheard.

My mother explained later that she had made a conscious decision not to tell us about seasickness in order not to put the idea into our suggestible minds. She was testing the hypothesis that most people would not feel seasick if they weren't expecting to.

But I remember that at the time, when my little brother and I felt so miserably ill, a terrible suspicion occurred to me. I didn't tell Martin about it because I didn't want to frighten him: but it quickly grew, like a balloon filled up with helium, into a certainty. The poison had been put into our food with our parents' knowledge, in order to get rid of us.

How did such an idea arise out of a childhood of which I retain only happy, innocent memories? We did not have a television, there was no way for gory tabloid stories to enter our imaginations. But I had a sense that when my parents went out at night, when my mother's face was pale with powder and fragrant with lipstick and perfume, when my father put on a starched white shirt and a beautifully coloured silk tie, they were really altered in a way that was significant. They were entering another sphere to which children were not admitted. I sensed an excitement and an anticipation in them that they were trying to conceal from us. The lipstick and the ornate hair clasps that my mother wore on such occasions made her look so beautiful. I guessed then that being parents was only one side of their nature.

That evening, it seemed clear to me that they were tired of our family life. We shackled them: they wanted to be free. The whole story about moving to Germany had been an elaborate deceit, a plan to lure us onto this ship where the cook and the stewards were already primed to put poison into our first night's dinner.

When my parents returned very late that night, my mother said, 'Oh, poor babies,' and fussed over us and soothed us while at the same time explaining about seasickness. Perhaps she gave us something to make us feel better, or perhaps her presence was enough to reassure us because by now, once our fear had abated, we didn't really feel so bad any more.

*

It seemed that fear came naturally to us children. On this same ship voyage, Martin, who was three, suffered agonies over the games of ping-pong that we played on deck. While my father taught me how to play, my brother sobbed with helpless terror. He was imagining the feather-light little ball flying over the railing, imagining himself as that little ball. My fear, which has stayed with me in one form or another throughout my life, involved the suspicion that the reality that was presented to me was a fabrication, an artifice made to conceal another, unknown reality, less friendly and secure, that lurked behind it. Even as I allowed myself to be comforted by my mother there was still a part of me that believed her capable of deceiving me. Every evening for the remainder of the voyage, when my parents attended their festive dinners and dances, I would lie awake hour after hour, listening intently for the sound of the helicopter or the little motor boat that was coming to carry them away.

4

SILKE'S HOUSE is only a few blocks away from where we lived after we came to Germany. Her furnishing is modern and the living room is light and spacious. All around are paintings and sculptures, heirlooms from a tobacco fortune. There are some things, too, that are very familiar to me, that used to be in our old apartment; and on one wall hangs a painting by my brother, white and silvery. Silke bought paintings from my brother before anyone else did. Silke has made coffee and tea and the three of us sit around the coffee table talking. 'You should open the gifts Irene brought us,' she tells my father. I watch uneasily as he unwraps first the jar of Connecticut honey and then the Mexican *salsa verde* with great ceremony. I feel embarrassed by these puny gifts, which were a last-minute thought. They both make a fuss, exclaiming that I shouldn't have carried such heavy items all the way across the Atlantic. Wanting to show his appreciation, my father jumps up and gets a spoon from the kitchen. He eats a spoonful of salsa out of the jar, then licks the spoon and dips it into the honey. 'It's *wonderful*,' he says. 'The salsa is incredibly hot, I love it.' By now I am squirming. Silke says, smiling, 'I look forward to trying the honey tomorrow morning at breakfast.'

When I visit my father and Silke there is always this sense that they are catering to me. I am subtly seduced, corrupted by it. I've come to feel it is my due. In conversations, everything I say is received uncritically, as if judgement could only be passed by me upon them, but not vice versa. I have a sick feeling of talking too much. At the back of my mind I suddenly have a vision of myself jabbering like someone possessed, saying anything at all, my mouth moving quickly, my eyes shining with an insane conviction of what I am saying.

Since moving to America I've visited them every few years. My father sends me cheques that allow me to travel to Europe and I reduce the portion of time that I spend with him to a minimum, a couple of days, a week at the most. Even so I feel I am doing him a favour. I've become a kept daughter.

But this time is different. I've paid for the tickets myself. I wanted to see him.

*

I don't remember being shocked when my mother told me that my father was having an affair. The surprise was that it was Silke. I knew that my mother had been nurturing suspicions about another laboratory associate named Connie. Once she had described to me in venomous tones Connie's flirtatious, kittenish behaviour, her little-girl's voice, her clinging mohair sweaters and her strong perfumes. But it wasn't Connie at all. It was Silke.

I was very young when I saw Silke for the first time. It was summer, shortly after our arrival in Germany. There was a party in someone's garden; Silke came late with her husband. She was wearing a miniskirt, showing her long tanned legs. I remember thinking her extremely beautiful, being astonished that such a fashionable woman could be a scientist.

Silke is tall and broad-shouldered and wears her thick dark hair long down her back; she seems to carry herself with a proud consciousness of its weight. When I met her again later, I buried the memory of my admiration like a guilty secret. I despised her. She was from Hamburg: I associated cold, aquatic traits with Germans from the far North. I felt contempt for her because she was rich, because she wore flowing skirts and delicately clinking bracelets, because her elegance intimidated me. I felt contempt for her because of her high voice, her feminine way of speaking, in sinuous cadences. And because of the presents she was always sending me and my brother — because she was trying so hard.

The clothes my father wears these days, the trenchcoats, the pleated trousers that skilfully conceal his paunch; the cherry-coloured shirt and the jacket in yellow-and-black houndstooth: I find them ugly, vulgar, a little repulsive. They are 'not him'. Silke's taste is evident even in his socks, which have a design of sea horses woven into them. If you look closely at his glasses, the joints in the frame turn out to be tiny hands.

A few years ago I found in a catalogue an exact replica of his old Norwegian fisherman's sweater. I was overjoyed, and without thinking of the meaning of what I was doing, I bought it for him for Christmas. His response sounded wistful: 'You have found my old sweater, you remembered it.' Now suddenly I am struck by the cruelty of that gift.

Gradually, my father tells me, people at the university are beginning again to accept and return their invitations. For years, he and Silke lived practically as outcasts, shunned by former friends.

*

Brigitte and Stefan show up just before dinner time. They were still small when their father moved out and mine moved in; now they are sixteen and seventeen, almost adults. I've seen Silke's ex-husband Dieter a couple of times. He is much younger than my father; he seems vain and humourless, fish-eyed. My mother had heard from someone, before, that the children were terribly spoilt. When their parents took them on a road trip, she'd heard, they would keep Stefan and Brigitte quiet by throwing candy into the back seat every once in a while. Despite everything, I think that they have both turned out very nice. I've watched them grow up and I feel affectionate toward them; after all, we share an intimate link. It's more than that: I feel guilty, responsible somehow, as if he were my fault, as if I'd passed my father off onto them. I keep expecting them to dislike me, and I'm touched when it seems that they don't. They go to my old school and we talk about the teachers we've had in common.

After dinner Stefan and Brigitte go down to their rooms and my father, Silke and I sit around the coffee table again. Tut, the cat, is sleeping beside me. He is named after the Egyptian king Tutankhamen, but he has become so obese that it's difficult to see any vestige of the dignity that once earned him this name. His body spreads out on the white leather sofa, almost as wide as long. He purrs when I put my hand on him. My father opens another bottle of red wine and Silke puts out dishes filled with sweets, biscuits and chocolates. She has brought a basket of clean laundry, and as we talk she begins to sort it. Silke is able to do any kind of chore as if it were not a chore at all but part of the life of luxury that she leads. She manages, in the midst of her work, to give the impression of someone who doesn't know what work really means. I once saw her clean up Tut's diarrhoea, which stank so terribly that

I could not offer to help. At that moment she still looked elegant, as though it could not touch her.

Now I watch as she takes a single sock out of the basket; looks at it; inserts her hand inside it all the way down to the toe to get out the wrinkles; finally smoothes it out on her lap, plucking at it here and there to get it into the perfect shape of a foot. Then she does the same to its companion, places the two carefully one on top of the other, and folds them in half. She treats underwear the same way, smoothing and folding even my father's most ragged underpants as if they were precious embroidery.

We talk about my grandmother, and I ask about my aunts Erika and Hannelore, because I've heard that they have quarrelled and are no longer speaking to each other. 'Oh, that's all nonsense,' my father says impatiently. 'It's silly to dwell on such things and make them more important than they are. I've told them both they shouldn't be so silly.'

I look at Silke. She seems surprised that my father doesn't want to tell me the story.

5

RETURNING TO THE NEIGHBOURHOOD in which I used to live, I am always surprised how much the same it all looks. Emotions long forgotten come alive again at the sight of familiar buildings and streets. For a little while this gives me the illusion that my childhood is a place that I have left, but that remains there, intact.

I remember the day we arrived in our new home in Germany. My mother had sent boxes of English books ahead of us; they were waiting for me in my room. I had immediately opened one of the boxes and was sitting on the floor absorbed in a Nancy Drew mystery, when I heard a commotion at the window. I looked out: nothing. Then again! I heard muffled giggles, and a pair of puppets appeared at the bottom edge of the window, hopping about wildly before disappearing altogether amidst squeals of laughter. Bettina and Peter, greeting me. I tried to find a place to hide in our apartment, where I could continue reading in peace, without being seen from the windows. About half an hour later, I heard the high chime of our doorbell for the first time, and my mother came to say it was for me. She had to push me to go to the door. There stood a blond, thin boy, wordlessly stretching a lollipop in my direction. I took it equally wordlessly, we both smiled awkwardly, and I closed the door in his face. That was Hans. There were three other families in our apartment building; altogether we were ten children. Later that afternoon, I sat on the balcony above ours with Peter's sister Monika, both of us silently drawing with crayons. I drew a picture of the *Europa*.

I was tutored in German for a few weeks by a woman named Frau Latsch, who had formerly been a schoolteacher. She was tall and large-boned. The lessons took place at the dining-room table in the small apartment where she lived by herself. They were excruciating. One day I excused myself to go to the bathroom. From the toilet my gaze fell on a jar on the shelf to my right, practically in front of my nose. I took the lid off and found inside an entire collection of lipsticks in different colours. I counted them, there were eleven. I couldn't believe it: my mother had only one lipstick! After washing my hands I couldn't resist the temptation to try one of them on in front of the mirror. I picked the most garish orange colour. Then I rubbed it off quickly with a tissue and tried a pink one, rich, sticky and perfumed. Now I had to try them all. There was something about the eleven different colours, like a new set of magic markers or crayons, that wouldn't allow me to rest until I'd tried each and every one of them. I worked feverishly, compulsively, scarcely taking the time to appreciate the effect of an individual colour. I used dozens of tissues; the whole area around my mouth was red and chafed from all the rubbing. Every now and then I flushed the toilet to mislead Frau Latsch.

After a while she must have begun to wonder what was taking me so long. She started calling me: 'Are you coming? Are you finished?' – 'Yes! Just a minute!' I yelled back. I was indignant: how rude of her to disturb me in the sacred privacy of the bathroom! I remember feeling completely free and secure in that locked space, where nobody's eyes could follow me. Because I had observed the way adults pretended not to notice when one of them left to use the toilet, I felt that I was in a sort of pocket sequestered from the normal course of time, and that when I came back out, it would be as if I had only been away for a minute.

It's not until I've tried on all of the eleven lipsticks, as I am working with soap, water and tissue to remove the traces of the last, that the realization hits me I am going to be in trouble.

*

My mother placed an advertisement in the newspaper and our family gained a new member, Frau Blume. Frau Blume was in her sixties, short and round, with big chipmunk cheeks and a friendly, turned-up nose. Because she liked to spend her afternoons on a towel by the lake, she was always tanned. She had been a nurse until her retirement, and before that, long ago in Poland, she used to be a nanny in a rich house. Once, too, even longer ago, she had had a husband; but he was a sailor and he died at sea after they had been married only a few months.

My mother worked half-days in the laboratory and Frau Blume came in the mornings. She cooked lunch and on Wednesdays she did the laundry. We never called her anything but Frau Blume and always used the polite form of address; but she was more like a grandmother than a babysitter or housekeeper. It was hard to believe that Frau Blume had not been cooking all her life. She seemed to live for our praise. She played the role of the *Hausfrau* to perfection, pressing us to eat more. 'There will be bad weather tomorrow if we don't finish it all up,' was her favourite threat.

My father would rather have stayed in the lab than come home for lunch. He preferred the American way, just a sandwich at noontime so that the day's work was not interrupted. He could easily have skipped the meal altogether. He ate absent-mindedly and Frau Blume kept having to recall him to the matter at hand: 'How do you like the dumplings, Herr Professor? Why don't you take a little more fat, Herr Professor, it makes it taste better. And you're sooo thin.' The cajoling cadence, the pouting look if the food was turned down, suggesting 'thankless sacrifice', were all part of an ancient repertoire.

One of the things my father hated most in life was to be pressed to eat more. Being 'urged' made him feel cornered. He had only two options: to stuff himself to the point of nausea, or to say no, to disappoint, to bring down on himself the resentment of the *Hausfrau*, who would take it as a personal insult to her cooking. Frau Blume, who couldn't help herself, who, if you'd gagged her, would still somehow have managed to squeak out, 'Have a little more,' provoked startlingly vehement reactions from my father every time he came home for lunch. He flared up. Precisely because he hated to say no, he said it all the more dramatically, with exasperation, his voice hoarse in a sort of suppressed shout: 'No!! I already said I don't want any more!'

There was a silence, and then, unsuppressible, Frau Blume would come back with something like, 'But you're thin as a *rail*, Herr Professor. You're like a skeleton! What harm could it do? I just want the best for you!' It made me want to giggle, both at Frau Blume's obtuseness and at my father, whose anger was of so little consequence.

Now, of course, my father had become the principal object of Frau Blume's attentions, her biggest challenge. To overcome

Herr Professor's indifference, to cook something that will send him into raptures, make him beg for more: it's not for us children that she comes early and spends hours in the laborious preparation of 'green dumplings', a dish that, like pickled *matjes* herring with potatoes, will remind my father of his childhood in Danzig. Danzig, now Gdansk, even then part Polish: Frau Blume used her unique link with my father to greatest possible effect. 'Don't you remember green dumplings?' My mother was her accomplice. Each morning my parents had this discussion: would he be able to come home for lunch today? It should be possible, there is no big experiment planned. And Frau Blume is going to make green dumplings. My mother placed the greatest importance on all meals being taken together as a family: we were not the kind of family where people came and went and ate as they pleased. Only the most stringent excuse, such as a Big Experiment, could release one from this obligation.

And Frau Blume has caught on to my father's taste. There are some things, after all, that pique his appetite, and better yet, that my mother wouldn't dream of cooking, that he can get only from his dear Frau Blume. Things that are edible only by a stretch of the imagination, organs of every description: kidneys, tongue, liver, tripe, spleen. It means she has to cook two meals, because of course my brother and I refuse to touch such things. The worst are the times, fortunately not frequent, when Frau Blume cooks kidneys for my father. Then the entire apartment smells like a urinal.

On nice summer days Frau Blume would take Martin and me to the shore with her. We spent the afternoons swimming in the lake and playing canasta afterwards in the sun, slathered with lotion, eating the snacks we had brought. My parents went on trips by themselves sometimes and then Frau Blume stayed with us. We ate scrambled eggs with chives for dinner and she baked huge sheets of crumb cake. She slept in my father's bed, snoring so loudly that I'd get up in the night and watch her for minutes on end, fascinated.

My parents subscribed to serious magazines such as *National Geographic* and *Scientific American*; but once a week, Frau Blume brought us her old issue of *Bunte Illustrierte*, a magazine filled with colour photographs. My father, my brother and I pounced on it. We fought over who could have it first. In it we read about all the celebrities and royalty: Udo Jürgens, Jackie Onassis, Romy Schneider; Count Rainier and Queen Sylvia and Princess Anne; but also about serial murderers and dogs that bit children to death.

※　※　※

When they were first married my parents shared five pairs of socks between them, they had almost no furniture, and the first big acquisition they made with the money they had saved was an old globe that they had seen in an antique shop. Our apartment represented the logical extension of that early choice. It was filled with paintings and antique furniture, pre-Columbian sculptures, old globes and microscopes; and at the same time there was an odd dinginess about it, a neglect of anything purely utilitarian. My mother had frugal instincts. She sewed all of her own clothes and mine, lengthened my brother's trousers year after year by adding on strips of cloth, hoarded in our basement stocks of food bought on sale. The floors were covered with our old shaggy blue carpeting brought from America; the curtains were made of cheap cloth. When my parents bought an antique, it had nothing to do with contemptible 'materialism'. It was a love affair, a joint fling.

33

Almost always it was love at first sight — some inexpressible quality of an object seen at an antique shop or auction (they put themselves in the way of temptation) would call out to them and from that moment on they talked about it incessantly, drew out the delicious agony of desire, guilt and indecision. They yearned for this thing, they had 'butterflies' of trepidation. And then one day there it stands, or hangs, the new *toy*, the coveted piece that has nearly bankrupted them. My parents will stop to admire it a dozen times a day. They'll look at each other and smile as if they shared some intimate secret.

A prize possession was the enormous gothic clock that hung in our living room, made of blackest wrought-iron. It didn't even have a face, only wheels and teeth. My father wound it up carefully each night, it was his ritual, pulling up the weights on their thick ropes. We were so used to it that we didn't hear it any more, but people told us its gong could be heard blocks away. It proclaimed our presence to the world.

*

Monika is my best friend. We are enraptured by anything Oriental. We play with Japanese dolls named Little Peach and Plum Blossom and invite each other to tea ceremonies with tiny messages written on rice paper: *Little Peach politely requests the pleasure of Plum Blossom's company for tea.* I have a table in my room devoted to my collection of every Asian object in the house I've been able to lay my hands on: starting with an Indian brass ashtray and two pairs of lacquered chopsticks. One day an Indian man named Herr Dasgupta sub-lets one of the apartments in the building and our excitement knows no bounds. We get up our courage and invite him very formally to tea in Monika's room. We put a tablecloth on her desk and bake a marble cake. Our efforts pay off: about a month later, before he leaves again, the kind man gives us each a real sari which his mother has sent from India. Thereafter we spend hours practising the folds, swathing ourselves in cool silk.

My wish for life is to become a Japanese monk-poet and write things that sound like this:

> *Long as the mountain pheasant's sweeping tail,*
> *the night, which I spend in solitude, stretches on.*

Sometimes it isn't Monika who is my best friend, but Bettina. In the garden there stands a metal frame meant for beating out carpets. It's perfect for climbing. We can hang upside-down by our knees, or else we perch on top, eating cherries and spitting the pits as far as we can.

On this day, because it is raining, we are inside drawing with pencils. Bettina says, 'Let's draw naked women.' I readily agree. 'Let's,' she says, 'not look at each other's pictures until they're done.' I understand the game. It's similar to playing with dolls: we are what we draw. I want my woman to be beautiful. I do my best to draw a beautiful naked woman like some pictures I've seen. I am shielding her with my left hand to protect my beauty secrets: long legs, the ideal curve of the hips, the breasts drawn as graceful shallow U-shapes with a lightly pencilled dot in the middle. When I'm finished Bettina is still working. Now that I am no longer preoccupied with my picture she seems even more anxious to conceal hers. The tip of her tongue comes out of her mouth as she concentrates fiercely, her left arm is curled round, her hair falls down from her bent head so that, however I try, I really can't see anything. I am worried. Why does she have so much to draw? Perhaps she's just slower, I comfort myself. I feel quite smug about my picture.

Finally she is done. 'You show yours first,' she says. 'No, you show yours first,' I respond automatically. The first rule of playing is symmetry. We unveil our drawings simultaneously and at that moment I realize that we've been playing different games. My woman is undoubtedly the better proportioned, but Bettina has given hers gruesome, embarrassing naturalistic details, hair at the crotch and little stipples around the central dot on the breast.

'My mother has these,' she insists triumphantly. 'Doesn't yours?' She presses me, but, frozen with shame, I refuse to admit anything of the sort.

*

Everyone says I look like my mother. I wish this were so, I wish I were beautiful like her; but if people looked again they'd see my father too. At first sight I am like my mother, but at second sight I am more like my father. It's the combination that's impossible: my face is crooked, odd, there is something bizarre about it. I can't believe it's really like that. Every time I look in the mirror I experience a shock of disgust and disappointment.

I decide that my mouth is the biggest problem. In front of the mirror I experiment and discover that I can change my smile by curling my upper lip under to make it thin. Bettina's family has invited me on an outing and I take the opportunity to practise my new smile. Bettina looks at me strangely, then asks me what's wrong. I pretend not to know what she's talking about. She takes me aside and whispers in my ear. 'I can understand if you're not in the mood to smile,' she says. 'I feel like that sometimes too. You don't have to smile if you don't want to. It's all right.'

I love nothing so much as being allowed to eat lunch with

Bettina's or Monika's family. Eating food that tastes different from what we eat at home is only the smallest part of the pleasure; I feel that I am tasting an entire existence that is radically unlike my own. I am envious of Bettina and Monika, not because I think their lives are better than mine, but because they live inside them, they know everything about them whereas I can only peek in.

I am nine or ten when I dream that I am caught snooping in Bettina's family's apartment. Nobody's home, the door was open and I have snuck in. Almost immediately I hear a noise: they're coming back. I'm trapped! I hide behind the sofa, in the closet; I crawl under the bed, flatten myself under the carpet under the bed. Frantically I try to do away with the evidence of my big body, to make it thin as the space behind the armoire, small enough to fit in a vase. All in vain. I wake up in terror just before the inevitable moment of discovery.

This memory haunts me for years. I am frightened by the obscure, guilty desire to trespass that has made a criminal of me in my dream.

*

Once, on a school holiday, Bettina and I amuse ourselves for a morning by taunting Frau Stadelhofer, the cleaning lady. Frau Stadelhofer is the story-book witch: with her scarf tied over her head like a hood, wisps of untidy grey hair coming out underneath; her hook nose with hideously stretched-out black nostrils; the long protruding tooth and the jutting chin. Only that she is quite tall, much larger than an ordinary witch. She is in her sixties and she lives in a farmhouse on the edge of town with her father. This concept is fantastic to me: that there can exist a man as much older than Frau Stadelhofer, who seems ancient, as my father is older than me. I imagine him as sightless, speechless and immobile, a monstrous being waiting for her at the kitchen table.

The town has grown around their farmhouse and the Stadelhofers' only produce are some potatoes that she brings to the weekly market on Saturdays. She has to walk the considerable distance on city streets, pulling her cart behind her. My mother sees her at the market, the smallest stand, nothing but a cartful of potatoes. Probably this is why we keep her on, even though she does not do a very good job cleaning.

Frau Stadelhofer is some sort of primitive relic. She has a strange gong-like voice and speaks an unmitigated version of the local dialect, which gives rise to endless hilarious imitations by us children. She hates the young people who hang about downtown with their motorbikes, and she'll say that Hitler wouldn't have stood for it. *Joh, joh, der Hitler het ufgrumt!* 'Yep, Hitler really cleaned up!' He would have taken the fire hose, she insists, and sprayed them all away. For her snack she requests a bottle of beer and some bread and *Wurst*. I sometimes spy on her discreetly as she sits by herself at the head of our table, chomping noisily and swilling the foul stuff.

Bettina and I call her Frau *Stinken*hofer. She really does smell very bad, and her smell lingers in our apartment for hours after she has left. On this day we have hit upon the idea of hiding behind furniture or doors as she moves around the apartment, and jumping out suddenly to startle her. The first time is a wonderful success, she yells and exclaims: *Jesses Maria und Josef!* After this we always give ourselves away by our giggling, we are laughing tears while she grows more and more frazzled. There is a helplessness about this witch. She is like some large dumb animal, and we are gadflies who won't leave her in peace.

*

At Christmas, when I am nine, there is a doll's house waiting for me under the tree. My parents have made it themselves, working on it in the evenings when we were asleep. It has three storeys, complete with stairs leading from one to the other, a terrace, a doorbell, and lights that work. Monika and Bettina and I play with it, dividing up the roles of the family members. In the family we play, the mother always has an impossibly high voice, with which she gives hysterical commands to the children: 'Clean up your room!' The children are spiteful, they fight with each other and throw things around. The father has a deep, growling voice; he is grumpy and wants to be left alone. Sometimes the children are beaten. We plunge our family with relish into the most awful scenes, the dolls in our hands jump up and down with excitement. What gives us these ideas? Our real families are nothing like this.

6

THE FIVE OF US – my father, Silke, Brigitte and Stefan and I
– get dressed up to go to a new Japanese restaurant that has
opened in town. The restaurant is attached to the town's most
expensive hotel, a former monastery by the lake. The name of
this hotel has an almost mythical resonance for me. In all the
years that I lived here, I never once set foot in it. I'm glad that
I've brought a skirt to wear, but I still feel badly dressed next
to Silke and Brigitte.

We park the car and walk across the gravel toward the
entrance, self-conscious in the spotlights that shine from
the building, an uneasy composite family. Brigitte breaks the
silence by joking that ours is the only 'ordinary' car among
all the Mercedeses and BMWs in the lot. My father says:
'When the university first invited me, they put me up in this
hotel.' And he describes how royally it was appointed. 'That
was when they were trying to lure me here. But ever since I
accepted the professorship, they have never again treated me
so well.' It's been so long since I've heard this comment that
I'd forgotten how predictably he used to make it. From the
silence of the others I know that they too have heard it more
than once.

We are seated around a large, circular table. Perhaps it's the way my father hails the Japanese waitress, or the imperious manner in which he opens his menu: I sense immediately the glum resignation that descends upon Stefan and Brigitte, see them hunker down in silent resistance. I see their instinctive premonition of another blighted evening, and I know exactly how they feel. My father seems all goodwill and cheerfulness, filled with a pleasurable excitement that he wants to communicate to the rest of us. 'What shall we get? Look, there's the sushi master, he is preparing it right over there in the corner! Do we all want *sake*? Ah, good, the waitress is bringing us some tea.'

There is an indefinable oddity about my father that becomes apparent when he is in public. He has lost a sense of himself. He speaks too loudly; his gestures are exaggerated. When I was small I was often embarrassed by his unusual behaviour, his indifference to appearances; but now, when I would be able to recognize this eccentricity as part of his charisma, part of what drew people to him, it has been superseded by a composite of slight dissonances that added together produce an eerie effect. It makes me feel ashamed of him, ashamed to be seen with him.

I wonder if he feels the hostility emanating from Stefan and Brigitte, if he feels his isolation as keenly as I feel it. Silke is doubtless used to these tensions, to mediating constantly between my father and her children. She is being silent now, perhaps hoping that my presence will help to smooth things over. I suddenly feel sorry for my father: it isn't right to let him be so outnumbered and isolated. So when he says, 'I want to go and watch the sushi master make our dinner,' I offer to accompany him. I am conscious of playing a role that is somehow expected of me – the loyal daughter. Silke expects it:

it buys her a certain reprieve. Stefan and Brigitte expect it too; it makes it all right for them to resent my father, since he has me.

I see the 'sushi master' smirk rudely at our approach. Then he pretends not to notice us as we stand, awkwardly and as if on display, watching over his shoulder as he slices the fish. This makes me angry. Out of what was merely an outward show of allegiance comes a genuine feeling of solidarity. I'm glad I've joined my father. After a few uncomfortable minutes he suggests that we go back to our table.

The waitress comes with a tray of *sake* jars. Bowing, she goes around the table to set one by each of our places. First me, then (skipping my father) Silke, then Brigitte, then Stefan – 'Hey!' says my father. 'What about me?'

'Oh—' The waitress looks in confusion from Stefan to my father, then blushes deeply and begins tittering. 'Oh, I'm sorry,' she stammers, 'I thought "Ladies first," I thought, because of his long hair . . .' She points at Stefan with his luxuriant mane and blushes some more.

Throughout the rest of the meal, my father gloats over this mishap. He brings it up again and again. He finds it irresistibly comic. He'll forget about it for a while and then suddenly it will occur to him again and he'll begin to laugh. 'She thought you were a woman!' Stefan says nothing; he can only glare back at my father, speechless and powerless.

I'd forgotten how vicious my father can be. The sympathy, however wary and hesitant, that I felt for him just minutes earlier has evaporated. And it seems to me, irrationally, that this is the real purpose behind my father's nastiness: as if he were twisting free from some kind of snare.

*

I remember once, when I was about seventeen, Stefan's age, sitting on our balcony at home. It was a beautiful sunny afternoon, the sky was clear blue and the geraniums in the balcony boxes were bright red and white. I'd made myself a cup of tea and was reading poems by Paul Celan. It's not enough to say I was reading: I loved Celan so much that I approached his poems, most of which I didn't understand, with a fervent expectancy, almost as if I could receive a sort of grace from them. There was one poem in particular which expressed, in such a cryptic and profound way that only I could understand it and my secret was safe, the way I felt about a certain boy.

My father came out onto the balcony. 'What are you reading?' He could tell I didn't want to talk to him. He pulled up a chair. 'What are the poems about? What do you like about them?' My monosyllabic responses were provoking him. He had all the time in the world.

'Give me an example. Show me one you like. What does it mean? Well, but what do you *think* it means? Aren't you capable of explaining this to me? It must mean something, if you like it so much.' I felt strangled by his questions.

In a way our roles have become reversed. My father keeps a distance now, barely dares to ask what I am doing, and I am the one who is curious. I want to know what goes on inside him, in the most private recesses of his consciousness.

7

In the evenings, when I was young, my parents always used to sit together in the living room. This was the constant, my whole life was contained within it; it had always been this way and it would last for ever. My mother sat in her favourite chair, reading peacefully in the lamplight. My father would sit on the sofa for a while, then get up and light his pipe and start pacing to and fro, to and fro, in front of the bookshelves. He was thinking. I never wondered what he was thinking about. If I had thought about it I would have said, 'His experiments.' He sometimes muttered to himself or laughed a little. If you addressed him while he was thinking, he'd look at you vaguely at first, as if it took him a few moments to come back.

My father charmed people. He made them feel that their lives were unusual and interesting. He told the car mechanic, the grocer who arranged his fruits with style: 'You are an artist!' And he meant it sincerely. He'd come back and tell us, 'That man is an artist.' A floor sweeper could be an artist if he swept with care and expertise and a certain élan. If all else failed, one could be a *Lebenskünstler*, an artist in living. Or perhaps that was the highest art of all.

He told Monika: 'You play the piano like a goddess.' He teased me: 'Monika plays the piano like a goddess.'

On Sundays, my father made soft-boiled eggs for breakfast. On school days my mother made fried eggs; but it was understood that only my father could make soft-boiled eggs just right. If my mother attempted it, they would end up either too hard or too soft. Even a timer wouldn't help her. It was an art, boiling eggs. When we cut them open, we raved with appreciation: 'Mine is just perfect!' 'Just *exactly* right!' 'To the second!' In our family, the most enthusiastic praise was merely common courtesy. My father himself was the greatest giver of compliments: he closed his eyes as he tasted my mother's sauce as if transported to seventh heaven; he pronounced it *divine, out of this world.*

My father only knew how to cook two things: soft-boiled eggs and scrambled eggs. He would tell us that as a student, after the war, all he ate was scrambled eggs, made from a powder which was his ration.

I loved the word my father used to express contempt for a person. *Dünnbrettbohrer*, a drill for thin boards, it said everything: a trivial person who expended energy on petty things, a person whose mind was fit only for light tasks. My father rarely expressed contempt, and when he did it was not with rancour but with mischievous relish.

My father was not like my friends' fathers, who were also professors, pompous and authoritative. My father was self-deprecating, apologetic. He liked to confess a weakness. Like Luther, he'd say, 'Here I stand, I can't help myself.' His weaknesses were: he lost his pipes, he forgot things. He didn't do things he'd promised to do.

He hated to have a time schedule: it was something that forced him to 'rush', to feel as if he were always too late, a

Hetze, as if dogs were chasing after him. My father had a fragile, precarious sense of personal freedom. An appointment, a social engagement, or a lecture obligation was a dark object blocking his view forward into the future; it became a hurdle he must cross, looming larger and larger as he approached it, filling him with dread.

'*Demands, demands, demands!*' he'd say, in English, as if there were no German word that adequately expressed such hatefulness. A responsibility meant that he had been boxed in, locked into a tiny space with no room for movement, no room to think. It meant that if he did not do a certain thing, there would be faces filled with disappointment and accusation. At such times it mattered little to whom these faces belonged. They were the enemy.

I was his friend: I said, 'Poor Papi.' He looked at me and smiled, both at me and at himself, ironically, because he liked that. It made him feel better. *Poor Papi!*

Every so often, he felt the need to wrench himself free. 'I won't do it!' he declared, with the same hoarse intensity with which he rejected Frau Blume's second helpings. 'I just won't! I refuse! Sometimes one has to defend oneself!'

I remember one morning my parents were having an argument before my brother and I left for school. They didn't quarrel often, but when they did it always seemed to me to be my mother who was angry, while my father was the one in need of sympathy and pity. My first class that day was a swimming lesson at the municipal pool and my mother had to drive me there. In the car she began to cry, asking me why I always sided with my father. 'It isn't fair.'

I was completely stunned. I had rarely seen my mother cry, and now she was bawling. And it was all my fault, for not loving her enough. Her weakness, breaking down instead of being angry and strong, made me see her point of view for the first time.

Still, a part of me continued to sympathize with my father. Almost certainly my mother was right and he was in the wrong; but I felt sorry for him just because of that. I could understand how bad it must feel to be wrong.

* * *

At the weekend my father and Silke take me on an outing to St Gallen, where we plan to visit the monastery library. My father has insisted that I sit in the front seat next to Silke, and he is sprawling luxuriously in the back. 'It's a whole new experience for me! I'm letting myself be chauffeured!' Along the way every once in a while he exclaims, '*Kinder*, what a beautiful day!'

In one of the towns along the way we see a circus procession: musicians, horses, elephants. The traffic is stopped and we watch the spectacle along with everyone else. It's a spontaneous street festival. When we can finally drive on we are all silent. The joyous fanfare seems to have had a depressing effect on my father.

It turns out the library is closed. We go instead to eat in an expensive restaurant, and afterwards we walk through the streets of the town. It's Sunday, and most of the shops are closed as well; but the jewellers have displays full of watches by all the famous Swiss makers. Silke and I tag along after my father as he looks in every window, glad that he is showing some interest.

I remember the time he bought himself a very sophisticated mechanical watch, that wound itself up by the natural move-ments of the wearer's hand. It had only a few seconds' deviation per year, and the deviation was constant. He was so excited about this acquisition, pondered and deliberated long in advance, that for days some mention of it was woven into every conversation. 'Do you want to know what time it is?' He would take any opportunity to push back his sleeve with comic ostentation and tell us *exactly* what time it was. It was a quite ordinary-looking watch, with a stainless steel case and band. Everything special about it was concealed on the inside, you had to know about it. And my father was delighted to explain.

It was similar with a sort of amulet he took to wearing later, a little brass ring that hung around his neck on a thin leather strap. He loved watching people's faces as they were put off at first by this piece of hippie-jewellery, and then asked, their curiosity getting the better of them: What is it? So that he could proudly say: 'It's a sundial,' and show them how there were actually two rings, one turning within the other, and engraved markings by which it was possible to tell the exact position of the sun. His own pleasure in the simplicity and clever functioning of this tiny scientific instrument was matched by his joy in showing it to people. He was a magician who transformed what looked at first sight like something from a hardware shop into a demonstration of human genius and cosmic precision. And then on top of that he had the gratification of seeing people's mocking smiles at his oddity turn into looks of admiration and stupefaction – because, despite his explanation, they still did not understand how the thing worked.

But now, as I watch my father hurrying from one window to the next, bending over the displays, he seems to me abstracted or deeply absorbed, as though he were not so much looking at the watches as searching in himself for his old interest that is lost.

8

I DREAM THAT we are hauling out of 'the cellar of the past' some old boots of my father's. There is a doorway, some steps leading down. I think it's my grandmother down there in the cellar, handing us up various items from the past. We take the boots from her hands. I understand vaguely that they're from 'the time of the war'. They're enormous: they're not so much boots as square red boxes. In fact they're a single box, subdivided into two compartments for the two feet. How could anyone walk in a single box? No, the box was not for walking, it was for the feet of soldiers who had fallen, I realize with a shudder.

But in reality my father was never a soldier. He was lucky.

*

My father: the little rich boy. Living in Oliva, a leafy suburb of the Baltic seaport of Danzig, the family had maids, a cook, a nanny. He remembers going one time with his mother to visit the Polish nanny on her birthday. They arrived at a dark, forbidding-looking apartment building. They rang, then stood waiting until she buzzed them in. Entering the dank hallway, they were assaulted by a strong odour. My father piped up in his high, childish voice: 'What's that smell?' 'Sshhh,' my grandmother shushed him. She whispered: '*Das ist Arme-Leute-Geruch*': poor people's smell.

My father became aware from early on that people were divided into those who were more lucky and those who were less lucky; and that he belonged to the first group. At Christmas, when my father and his friends received wonderful presents, bicycles and toy trains and chemistry sets, the Polish children in his class at school would get only a few oranges or nuts.

At an age when other boys were acquiring their vocabularies of dirty words, my father was memorizing the names of protozoa: *Actinophrys, Pelomyxa, Globigerina*. Later, when the war had already started, he kept an ant colony in a container bounded by sheets of glass, so that he could observe the activity of the workers. He cultured bacteria in petri dishes; throughout the night he'd get up secretly every few hours to chart their growth. He even had a pet spider; it was striped, and was called a Harlequin Jumping Spider.

Towards the end of the war there began to be severe food shortages in most German cities; but Danzig, because of its geographical isolation, was spared this hardship. Its markets were still filled with fat geese and juicy blueberries from the surrounding countryside.

February of 1945. I have often heard this story from my father. My grandfather, a banker, had been called up to the Eastern Front the previous year; but he had an administrative post close to Danzig and came home at weekends. That winter had been a bitterly cold one. Coal was in short supply, the central heating could no longer be used in all the bedrooms; so my father slept in the living room, where there was a tiled wood stove. The family radio was also in this room, and he began to listen at night to the BBC's German broadcast.

Listening to enemy broadcasts, and especially telling others about them, was a crime punishable by death. Therefore he was afraid to tell even his mother when he heard about the Conference of Yalta, in which it was decided how Germany was going to be divided up. He had just turned sixteen, and he went around keeping this secret to himself: that the war was almost over and their home would go to Poland and they would have to flee.

When the day came, my father says now, it was all so ordinary. He simply went to the train station and bought tickets. Four of them: for himself, his mother, and his two younger sisters Hannelore and Erika. His father was staying behind. The train they got on was one of the last to leave the city. Officially it was carrying military supplies to the west of Germany, but in reality it was filled with the families of high-ranking officials, escaping days before the arrival of the Russians. There was a snowstorm the day they left. An icy wind blew flurries across the platform. My grandfather made sure they were comfortably settled, then he got off and waved as the train pulled away.

They travelled endlessly, changing trains, struggling up and down underpasses, my younger aunt, Erika, continually crying *Mila, Mila,* wanting milk. My grandmother wore her fur coat, carrying in its pockets tens of thousands of marks, the entire contents of their bank account, worth nothing. Travelling separately by ship were sixteen wooden crates that had been packed in haste, containing all valuable or useful belongings, silver, paintings, children's toys.

Of these crates only one ever arrived. A large ship had left Danzig around the same time, filled with refugees who were not able to leave by train, was sunk; perhaps the crates had been on this ship. The one crate that did arrive was filled with oatmeal. My father remembers eating the musty cereal for months afterwards.

But the only thing he cared about, my father will say, 'the only thing that mattered to me, was my microscope.' He still has this microscope; I've seen it. It has a beautiful mahogany case, with a carrying handle and a simple, neat latch; when you open it, it folds apart into two halves, with moulded hollows lined in blue velvet for each of the parts of the instrument. The case itself is the embodiment of all the covetous, anxious care with which a precious possession might be surrounded. Outside a strongbox, sharp-edged, giving nothing away; inside, all delicate softness and shock-resistant cushioning, like the inside of an egg. My father had not allowed his microscope to be packed in the crates along with everything else, but had insisted on carrying it the whole way.

My father was lucky for this reason: if he had been born only seven days earlier, on the last day of 1928 instead of on 6 January 1929, he would have been drafted at the beginning of 1944, along with many of his classmates whose sixteenth birthdays fell in that year. If he had been born seven days earlier, he wouldn't have been there to make the long train journey with his mother and his sisters. My father's cousin Karl, only a few weeks older than he, ended up a prisoner in France under conditions so harsh that he died of a weakened heart soon after the war.

*

They made their way to Southern Germany, to stay with my grandfather's family in a muddy village in Swabia. My grandmother had never met these people before; she knew next to nothing of her husband's background. They were peasants, and they resented my grandmother with her fur coat and superior manners. My grandmother, for her part, would always say contemptuously that Swabians could not be clean, since they used their bathtubs to store potatoes. This family was shot through with a streak of brooding and tragedy. My great-grandfather had hanged himself in his own barn, and two of my grandfather's sisters had drowned themselves, one in Lake Constance and the other in a nearby pond. *Sie gingen ins Wasser*, 'they went into the water': the phrase in which these two separate acts have become framed seems to suggest that there was something romantic about it, that they wore white gowns and went slowly, singing, looking straight ahead.

My father would later tell my mother about these suicides with a sort of pride, as if hinting at a hidden dark side in his own nature.

Although the war was all but lost, the military leadership continued recruiting young boys to the very end, feeding them to enemy artillery in a frenzied last effort. In March, soon after their arrival in Southern Germany, my father received his draft notice from the regional *Jungstammführer*. '*Hitlerjunge* Christof!' the letter began.

It continued something like this: 'It is time for you to join the struggle. You are hereby requested to present yourself at headquarters in one week's time, equipped with provisions sufficient for three days and the following items . . .' There followed the kind of packing list that might be given to a boy going to summer camp – socks, toothbrush, soap, towel, anorak. The letter was signed: '*Heil Hitler!* Sincerely yours, *Jungstammführer*———.'

My father always says that the part about bringing provisions for three days sounded like a joke. People were scraping by from one day to the next and there was never any extra food.

He wrote the following letter back: 'Dear *Jungstamm-führer*———! I am eager to join the struggle. Unfortunately, I have a bad sore throat and have to stay in bed. As soon as I get better, I will present myself at headquarters as requested. *Heil Hitler!* Sincerely yours, *Hitlerjunge* Christof.'

This letter was of course the height of audacity. He could have been court-martialled for putting forward such a ridiculous excuse. His gamble was that the letter would be lost or at least delayed in the general disarray of things, that the war would be over before it reached its destination.

But the postal system was evidently functioning perfectly, for the response arrived in the mail three days later. Fear coagulated in the pit of his stomach as he tore open the envelope, certain that he was going to be called to account for his treasonous impudence.

It was a very short note. '*Hitlerjunge* Christof! I have received your letter and am sorry to hear that you are unwell. I hope you feel better soon. *Heil Hitler!* Sincerely yours, *Jungstammführer*———.'

The recruiter, knowing as well as my father that the war was already lost, had simply decided to let the matter go.

*

Most of the time, when I heard this story, I heard in it my father's pride over his own cheek, how he had made his own crazy luck by a schoolboy prank. That letter he wrote was a daring, reckless gesture like tossing a die with everything to lose. And he won!

But sometimes it sounded a little different to me. There was another emotion, too: a kind of stricken astonishment, even after all these years, at the *Jungstammführer*'s response, that small, human voice coming from within the Nazi machinery. This person whom my father did not know, and who owed him nothing, had saved his life. The letter that came back to him was like a friendly wink, only that his friend never materialized, there was no one to be grateful to, and my father was left alone with his cleverness, his luck.

I think he told the story with something like shame, never failing to bring up his cousin Karl who was not so lucky, as if he felt himself the beneficiary of a monstrous unfairness.

9

I AM TAKING THE TRAIN to Stuttgart, to stay with my aunt Erika and visit my grandmother in her retirement home. I am worried about how I will find my grandmother.

While taking me to the train station, Silke has told me about the quarrel between my aunts. About a year ago, Hannelore came from Frankfurt to visit my grandmother and found her little apartment sadly out of order. Dirty stockings stashed in the desk drawer, unwashed dishes on the windowsill. Until then, no one had noticed any sign of my grandmother's mental decline. Hannelore accused Erika of neglect: how could she have been unaware of what was happening? In her busy way, she set about having things washed, labelling the shelves in my grandmother's closet and giving instructions to the staff. Upon her return to Frankfurt, she fired off a letter to Erika filled with more instructions. Naturally Erika was deeply offended; living so close to my grandmother, she visits her far more frequently than either of her siblings. Since then they have only communicated by mail or by giving messages to each other's husbands.

The notion of my two aunts not getting along is still almost inconceivable to me. Until now I've always thought of them in one breath, Erika and Hannelore. Hannelore dark-haired and petite, Erika fair and tall, willowy: just because they're so different they seem to belong together. Erika, the younger one, is a painter. She paints sheaves of flowing parallel lines that puncture the surface on which they are drawn and continue on the other side, or that reach the edge of the paper or canvas and, turning an infinitesimal corner, pursue their course on its reverse; she sews beautiful books in which the lines travel from page to page. Erika, distracted, might have seen a stocking leg hanging from a desk drawer and thought nothing of it, whereas to Hannelore, who is more observant, it was a signal for alarm. Hannelore is emotional, watchful, high-strung; she was older when the family fled Danzig and she feels bereft, suffers from her memories. I imagine that in accusing Erika of neglect, she may have been giving vent to some grievance whose roots went deep into the past.

Looking out the window of the train, I see blossoming meadows and orchards. At one point there is a fox bounding through the grass. Even at a considerable distance and despite the train's motion, I can make it out clearly, a reddish fox. It is sharp and precise and looks – I've never seen one before – just like the ones drawn in fairy tale books.

Later, the orchards are replaced by tall, dense pine woods: we are going through the Black Forest.

I find myself remembering a peculiar scene that I witnessed the last time I visited my grandmother. She had invited me, as usual, for a *Mittagessen* in the restaurant downstairs. An old lady was sitting at the table next to ours, and the new manager of the restaurant came personally to take her order. I couldn't help staring and listening, with a mixture of repulsion and fascination, as he paid her court.

'And what will we have today?' His voice oozed ingratiat-
ingly and his sausage fingers twiddled nervously as he spoke.
He was heavy-set, close to fifty, with an orangish complexion
and pomaded hair. 'Shall we make you a lovely beef roulade
with a wonderful little sauce, the way you like it? Some nice
potatoes to soak up the sauce?'

The lady seemed ancient: she had a transparent halo of
silver hair and a thickly painted, wrinkled face. Though she
responded archly to the manager's attentions, it was clear that
she was pleased and flattered by them. Like a countess and her
lackey: the lackey, bulging out of his suit, fattened on her pantry,
revealing a calculating contempt for his weak and trembling
mistress by the excessive affectation of politeness that was
exaggerated beyond all credibility. At the same time there
was something desperate about the man, as if he were clinging
to his customer's willingness to buy his little act, pitiful as it
was. He had only recently taken over this establishment. A
ghost of failure seemed already to hang about him.

He put the old lady's dinner down before her with extrava-
gant wishes for her enjoyment and good digestion. He was on
the point of leaving again, but then he stopped short as if hit
by a sudden thought and turned around on his toes like a
dancer.

'You know,' he began, 'I am particularly glad to see you
here again today.' The old lady acknowledged the compliment
with a little smile, her fork and knife already poised over the
roulade. 'Because as I remember now, wasn't there something
wrong with your fish the last time you were here? I am very
glad that—'

'Oh no, that was a long time ago.' The lady waved him off.
'I've been here several times since then.'

There was a strange look on the manager's face, which might have been embarrassment over his mistake. 'No,' he said slowly, as if thinking very hard, 'I'm sure it was the last time you were here, I remember clearly about the fish. There was something wrong with it—'

'I've been here since then,' she repeated, impatient to begin eating now. 'You just don't remember.'

'No, no,' the manager insisted, with an obstinacy that was becoming ludicrous and at the same time sinister. 'It was the last time. I am quite sure of it.'

I was stunned by the barely concealed brutality of it. Rather than relinquish his claim to perfect recollection, which must have been, in his own mind, the cornerstone of his success with his clientele, the manager was determined to shake the old lady's certainty by sheer force of assertion – to arm-wrestle her into acquiescence by the superior power of his younger mind over her older one. It was as if he were testing the theory that the reality in which old people lived was an infirm, malleable one, and that in the end they had little choice but to accept the story that one handed to them.

My grandmother was too well bred to stare at other people, however surreptitiously, or listen to their conversations. She waited politely for my distraction to end so that we could talk together.

In all the years, my grandmother never seemed to me to change at all. I think of her as dignified and full of politeness; a solidly framed person with a broad, friendly face. Wearing silk blouses with small geometric prints, in greens and browns and blues; a bow at the neck, a discreet brooch. Nothing floral or overly feminine; no warm colours. I think of how she used to read *Spiegel* magazine dutifully, from cover to cover; whistled tunelessly to herself when she was nervous. Her short hair went so gradually from black to grey to white that I never noticed it happen.

✻

The retirement home consists of three ugly high-rise towers. My grandmother planned her own transfer to this place many years in advance, putting aside money for it when she was still in her fifties, as if she could not wait to grow old. It is one of the more expensive establishments in Germany, with spacious, well-kept grounds. The residents have every convenience, there are 'cultural events' and bus outings into the countryside each weekend. On the inside it's like a carpeted prison, hundreds of doors all alike. My grandmother's door is number 3116: the sixth door on the eleventh floor of the third tower.

Encountering residents in the hallways and lift, I experience what it is like to be a thug. In proximity with their frailty I feel my own youth and vigour as threatening – although I am not especially big or strong. The idea of violence somehow suggests itself. How easy it would be to knock someone over, grab a purse out of some nice lady's hand. There is shockingly little security. I wonder if they are worrying about this as they look at me.

As I approach my grandmother's door, I am nervous. Erika has given me the key, saying that she won't necessarily open up to me. 'You ring the bell and she'll say *Yes*, and you'll stand there expecting her to appear any minute – but she doesn't.' So I ring the bell and immediately bend over and start fumbling with the lock. Like a thief. I look up and down the hall to see if anyone is watching me.

Oh, is it locked? I hear. *Just a minute, I'm coming.* And then my grandmother opens the door.

'Großmutti!' I am prepared for non-recognition. She looks at me, I look at her. 'It's me, Irene.'

She starts to close the door again, withdrawing behind it, perhaps fearfully, I think, or suspiciously. Then she pulls it open again, apparently recognizing me after all. 'Oh, Irene! How nice that you're coming to visit me!' I gently, carefully, hug and kiss her.

The first thing I notice on entering the room is the bad smell, as if the toilet hadn't been flushed. But as I step farther in, I realize it is worse than that.

There are faeces all over the floor. Smeared over the rugs, spread across a large area, near the kitchenette and in front of the bookcase filled with familiar volumes, hardback editions of Thomas Mann, Günter Grass and Max Frisch. My grand-mother herself is clean, nicely dressed. She doesn't show any awareness of anything out of order. The only thing I can do is to ignore it as well. I step around the worst spots. She sits down in her armchair and I sit next to her and we begin our conversation.

We sit with our hands folded politely and converse. We sat in just the same way when I last visited her, when she was in fine health, went swimming every morning in the indoor pool. But now it is obvious that she is unwell; her lips are white and she seems weak.

Her first question to me: 'When were you born?'

'Nineteen-sixty?' she exclaims when I tell her. 'Imagine! I was born in nineteen-six!' After a minute she asks me the same question again, in the same curious tone, and I try to respond as if she had just asked it for the first time.

'In nineteen-sixty? Isn't that something! And I, in nineteen-six.'

I have time to wonder whether she is remarking on the

inversion in the two dates, or on our difference in age. I have the feeling it is neither, so much as that she is holding the two figures side by side, making an effort to bring them into some relation. As if all the numbers in between had dropped away and there were only these two left, hers and mine, floating in the universe at a great distance from one another.

The question and answer have something childlike, as if we were little girls exchanging as intimate confidences the simple facts of our lives. Hers and mine. A wave of tenderness comes over me.

'And I was born in nineteen-six. Well, then I have a right to just sit around here all day long, don't I? Who would have thought that it would end like this . . .'

This is said with a smile, a touch of humour. It is the closest my grandmother, who never tolerated complaining either in herself or in others, will ever come to expressing distress. And several times during our conversation, which circles slowly and is filled with silences, she returns to a variant of this sentiment, though always with the same mild smile.

'And then you just sit around all day long . . . How lucky that one doesn't know in advance how one's life is going to end up one day.'

What do I really know about my grandmother? When I was born, it was already long after she had been, as she herself liked to put it, 'plucked' by life. She often used this expression: 'plucked'. She did not mean as a flower is plucked, but as the feathers are plucked from a fowl.

We used to visit her after she'd moved to Munich. We took walks to Nymphenburg Park, and she used to carry Emser salt tablets in the pocket of her light-coloured raincoat, and a second pillbox containing little squares of chocolate that she offered us 'for energy'. At breakfast she would remove the soft insides of her rolls, the part I loved best, and discard them by the side of her plate. I am telling my grandmother about these things that I remember: the 'Toast Hawaii', with ham and pineapple, that she used to make for dinner; the gas water-heater in her bathroom that roared softly while you sat in the tub.

She looks blank, bored. Finally I ask her outright: 'Do you remember living in Munich?'

'Oh yes, of course . . .' She realizes that I require proof. 'It was a nice city to live in – good theatre, and of course the woods and the mountains nearby. The Baltic, which was warmer than the North Sea, you could swim in it . . .' She is remembering not Munich but Danzig, many years earlier. 'There was a dumb waiter, I remember, on which the cook used to send up the food from the kitchen downstairs. A little bell rang when it arrived.' She laughs a little and seems to relax, pleased that she has been able to pass my test.

I feel guilty for having subjected her to it.

At the same time I feel a subtle excitement. An idea is taking shape, I begin to perceive a unique opportunity. Whatever passes between us will never come to light, it will never go beyond this room. My grandmother herself will not remember it: it will be erased, as if it never happened. For the first time in my life I can ask her anything I want. There is something frightening about this. But I am curious. I want to ask her the kind of questions that you are never allowed to ask another person. I want to wrest from her not her pocketbook but her most private thoughts, her secrets.

*

My grandmother has always kept her secrets. During the Third Reich she kept a secret from her husband, her children, from

63

everybody. She was one-eighth Jewish. She trembled at the thought of the disgrace she would bring upon her family if it was discovered.

I could never ask my grandmother questions about this time. What did she see, what did she know, what did she think? 'I'd rather not talk about it,' she'd say. And sometimes she'd add something about having been 'plucked'.

And what about my grandfather? What was he like? How did she feel about him?

My aunt Erika has told me the story of how they met.

It was 1927, my grandmother was twenty-one years old; she lived with her stepmother in Plauen. She was vacationing by herself at the fashionable spa of Bad Reichenhall in Bavaria. I picture the place like something out of Thomas Mann, elegantly clad guests strolling slowly down gravel paths, sketching or reading in the shade of broad-rimmed straw hats. In the afternoons you could visit an establishment called the *Tanzcafé*. A little band played light waltzes and couples danced on the honey-coloured parquet, while others sat at tables on the side drinking coffee or tea and eating petits fours. There was an atmosphere of lightness and gaiety, with sunlight streaming in through tall windows.

My grandmother was one of those sitting on the side. She had a book, in which she pretended to be immersed. All at once a gentleman whom she had noticed earlier, and who was also alone, came up to her and proposed a dance. They danced. When the dance was over, my grandmother excused herself and left. Erika says that she always finished her account of the incident with these words: 'Afterwards, of course, I left.'

Why 'of course'? Would it have been unseemly to stay? Would it have seemed too eager to have accepted a second dance? Or was it that she was afraid of not being asked a second time, of being left sitting alone again at her table, with her book? Or did she leave in order not to put her new acquaintance in the position of having to dance with her the rest of the afternoon, in case he didn't want to? Was she so flustered by the feelings aroused in her during that one dance that any more would have been too much?

Whatever the reason, my grandmother simply departed, leaving everything further up to chance. Perhaps they encountered each other here and there on the gravel paths. As her vacation came to an end and she was getting ready to leave, her gentleman acquaintance remarked that he had heard what a beautiful city Plauen was, and that he had always wanted to see it. He suggested that, when he himself travelled home to Danzig about a week later, he could interrupt his journey for a brief visit.

My grandfather would recount later that as his train approached Plauen, he told his fellow passengers: 'If she has come to the station to meet me, I will get off the train. If I don't see her there, I'll just keep going.'

My grandmother was, of course, waiting at the station. She was wearing a hat of which my grandfather would afterwards say: 'But I really didn't like that hat you had on!' She had booked a room for him in the best hotel and in general made flawless arrangements, avoiding any embarrassment. They visited the sights of the city. They were both orphans. He was, though not yet forty, a vice-president at his bank. Within a short time he had proposed to her and she had accepted.

What if they had not met again? What if, when the train pulled into the station of Plauen, my grandmother had been hidden by a crowd; or what if some accident had delayed her by as little as two minutes?

'Thus everything hung from a silken thread,' Erika said

when she had recounted this story to me; and her eyes were moist at the thought of it. Everything had depended on a chance so tenuous, so fragile; and if the thread did not break despite the tremendous weight that was appended to it, then, certainly, it was a marriage that was meant to be, a union made in heaven . . .

*

But my aunt's story, like all stories, like the phrase *Sie gingen ins Wasser*, is only a cover, a decoy, made to protect and seal up the truth. Perhaps my grandmother has forgotten the story now, and the questions I ask her will reveal something more, or something different. Would it even be wrong? Isn't it rather a matter of rescuing at the last moment some fragments of her life before they dissolve without a trace?

I want to know how she really, secretly, feels about us, her family. Does she guess that my two aunts have stopped speaking to each other since she became ill? Has she allowed herself to realize what has become of my father, her favourite?

But instead of letting me question her, my grandmother begins to question me. She seems to sense the experimental nature of our conversation, a licence of which she too can take advantage. Though her memory may be disintegrating, her intelligence in the present moment is not; if anything I feel it is more keen than ever. For months she has been misleading everyone as to the degree of erosion by carefully constructing a façade from moment to moment, deducing from hints what she ought to know. Now she lets down her bluff. She is avidly curious. Are her daughters married? What about her son?

Am I his daughter?

*

We are interrupted when the doorbell rings. A nurse enters briskly, carrying a lunch tray. She immediately takes me aside, nods at the carpet and says in a stage whisper: 'I've already notified the special cleaners. If only she'd leave those pads in . . .'

When the nurse has left my grandmother begins to apologize profusely: 'I'm sorry I have to eat now, in front of you. But you'll be eating something downstairs later, right? Together with the others? That will be nice, I'm sure you have a lot to tell each other.' And again: 'I'm so sorry I have to eat now, and you have nothing. But it's my duty, they're coming to take the tray soon, and this will have to last me until dinner. You'll be eating downstairs with the others, won't you?'

Her universe has become this simple: the others are 'downstairs', happily conversing, while she lives out her days in the solitude of her little room 'up here'. I don't contradict her. In the end, because she is truly distressed by the impoliteness of eating in front of me, I offer to eat her cucumber salad, which she doesn't like; and she seems happy, as if she were getting away with something.

We eat in silence. The effort to communicate is over. I know that this is our last meal together, I will not see my grandmother again. But the significance of this remains outside of me. My grandmother and I smile at each other like shy strangers.

Later a man comes with a special carpet-cleaning machine and the nurse takes the tray away again. My grandmother looks sleepy and I know it is time for her nap, time for me to leave. I adjust the reclining back of her chair and put the blanket over her, tucking her in like a child. I bend over and hug her awkwardly, kissing her on the cheek, and then we both say goodbye and I simply go out the door and close it as quietly as possible behind me.

As I walk down the hall, my hands retain the memory of the loose, soft feel of her shoulders when I embraced her, like something that slides and melts away at the touch.

*

Afterwards my aunt Erika and uncle Gerhard ask me about my visit. I hesitate a moment, then tell them unsparingly what I found. In retrospect I am angry that no one warned me. Both of their faces fall as if all the tension had suddenly gone out of them. They seem at once crestfallen and relieved by my bluntness. I have the impression they had both hoped and dreaded that I might say it outright.

My aunt tells me about my grandmother's brief stay in the hospital, during which her mental condition deteriorated considerably. The worst thing was the way the staff treated her, the rudeness, the disrespect, as if she were not a person. A couple of times Erika observed them when they didn't realize she was there.

'I'll never forget how she said goodbye to the nurses.' She seems to have to brace herself to continue. 'She had asked me, the day before her discharge, to bring something that she could give them as a little gift. So I went and got some expensive coffee, beautifully packaged. When I came to pick her up, the nurses were in their kitchenette, gossiping and laughing. She was all nicely dressed now, instead of her hospital shift she was wearing a suit and coat, with her hat and scarf and all. And she went up to these nurses, these same nurses who had treated her so awfully, and said, "I'd like you to have this as a token of my appreciation. You were so kind and made me feel so much at home during my stay here."

'Because, you see, she didn't remember that she hadn't been treated well.'

10

IT IS STILL DARK when we get up. Five o'clock. We get dressed, hollow-eyed, by lamplight. There is a strange, hushed atmosphere. My mother has a list of tasks to be done, things to be remembered, and she is already busy crossing items off by the time we are fully awake. From her master list she draws two smaller lists for me and for my brother: appliances, plants, trash, windows. We eat breakfast out of disposable plastic dishes so that no time will be wasted washing up. For some reason we are all whispering, as if we were leaving in secret.

My father has no list, he does not take part in this busyness and efficiency. He is responsible for only a few tasks, but large ones: fitting our luggage in the boot and on the roof of the car.

Then out into the raw early morning air. In the car we all have to wear helmets. We are four bubble-heads, two enormous red ones in front, two smaller ones, one white, one red, in the back seat. My parents wear serious mountain-climbing helmets; my brother and I, because we are less endangered, have a cheaper, department store version. There is only one other family in the world who wear helmets in the car: that of my aunt Erika. Onkel Gerhard is a doctor; he has seen many crash victims and he maintains that lives could be saved if people wore helmets.

The real function of the helmets seems to be to signal our abnormality as a family. My brother and I lower ourselves in the seat as we drive through the streets of our town, stop at the Swiss border for a passport check. My mother has come up with the idea of tying a scarf over her helmet, thinking that then it will appear as though she had a bouffant hairdo. But in combination with the large polaroid sunglasses that both she and my father wear, the scarf only makes her look even odder.

After a while, though, the farther we are from home, the less we are embarrassed. We stare back. These people by the side of the road and in the others cars mean nothing to us; we laugh to see their dumbfounded faces swivelling as we pass by. It's exhilarating to be odd, to be different. We're together in this, as a family.

The first part of the drive, through Switzerland into the Alps, is fun. As our journey progresses we can see the day progress. First there were only bakery trucks on the road; the traffic grows heavier and pedestrians more numerous in each town we pass through. At eight people are hurrying to work; by ten it's housewives, strolling leisurely on their shopping errands. Everywhere people are going about their usual routines; only we are not, we are temporarily on the outside of life, surveying it as we pass through.

We eat our sandwiches, our fruit, the cake my mother has packed, at some rest stop in the mountains, shivering in the cold air. After this there is nothing to look forward to. The second half of the trip is gruelling. The Italian *autostrada* is heavily travelled, filled with swaying trucks and Northern European vacationers converging into this one southbound channel.

The car soon becomes boiling hot, even with the roof open. A whole bag of gummi bears has melted and leaked onto the black plastic seat. My brother and I quarrel. Wrecked cars line the highway, multiple pile-ups, ghastly visions of crumpled and torn metal, ambulances coming to take away the bodies.

Now our helmets take on a new significance, underscoring the danger of such travel. The night before our trips I am always in an agony of terror, certain that this time we are going to die. Lying in bed I pray fervently, clenching my hands together, that we may be saved just one more time: 'Please, dear God.' The emptiness into which my prayer seems to fall intensifies my dread. I have to pray harder still: 'Please, please, please, please, please.' I am frantic, weeping. I am only able to calm down by making peace with the idea of dying, surrendering myself to fate. It doesn't matter. Whatever happens, happens. I won't know anything. I won't be around to miss anything.

The next morning my fears seem a little ridiculous. The reality isn't as bad as the anticipation. Even on the *autostrada* I only feel a constant, tense alertness, a rush of alarm each time my father goes into the passing lane or has to brake suddenly. My parents take turns driving, but he usually does this difficult part. Our lives are in his hands. He is a hero.

*

We spent a couple of summer vacations in Terenten, a village in the Tyrolean Alps. We stayed in a little *Pension*, slept under duvets, ate three-course dinners at our *Stammtisch*, and went on walks during the daytime that we called 'hikes'. There were goats and windmills on these hikes, flowers by the path and brooks with little waterfalls; my brother and I stood in our bathing suits underneath them, shrieking ecstatically. We had to drink disgusting milk with thick cream on top, still warm from the cow. One year I made a little friend in the village, Anne-Marie, who taught me how to say *Gute Nacht* in dialect.

But it was the family who ran the *Pension* that occupied most of my thoughts. The wife, Frau Theiner, did all the cooking in addition to taking care of her three or four little children; she looked harried, hollow-eyed with overwork. She had natural bright pink spots on her cheeks and her nose was often red, too, from crying. The husband, Herr Theiner, was a blacksmith. Every couple of days some farmer would bring his horse and we stood around watching as Herr Theiner hammered the horseshoes into shape on his anvil, the metal glowing red-hot, sparks flying, blows ringing out sharply. My father was excited, he filmed it. He said it was a dying art. I winced as the nails were pounded into the horse's hoof. Once Herr Theiner must have driven one into the flesh, for the horse went crazy and Herr Theiner, instead of being sorry, cursed brutally.

Herr Theiner was a horrible man. He was the first drunk I'd seen close-up. He'd appear in the early evening, shouting at his wife, bellowing out strings of abuse. I couldn't under-stand a word of it because it was in dialect, ugly drawn-out diphthongs and menacing gutturals, spit flying. The guests, if it happened to be dinner time, sat in stunned silence at their tables, listening to Frau Theiner's tearful attempts to hush him, appease him, or send him away. He never came into the dining room but glared resentfully in our direction as he stumped by the door. He smelt of manure; he was as crude and uncivilized as Frau Theiner was prim and refined, as if they belonged to different species. Finally she'd hasten in bearing our soups, our delicate dumplings floating in broth: 'Sorry to keep you waiting.' She seemed to be pleading for forgiveness, smiling bravely while her eyes were still brimming over.

My mother scoffed at Herr Theiner. She seized on the fact that he never took his hat off, even indoors, as a sign of his stupidity: 'His dunce cap, he wears it instead of a brain.' It was probably true that he was stupid, with that childish look in his dim eyes, the mouth curled to a permanent snarl, even when he smiled. But to me my mother's contempt seemed irrelevant; it certainly didn't lessen the horror of this man who was pure evil, whose nature was revealed in the murderous fury with which he swung out and struck down on the live, blazing metal on his anvil.

One night there was a thunderstorm and Frau Theiner was crying uncontrollably. She was terrified of the lightning. The year before a barn just up the road had burnt down, she explained.

I remember being amazed at this, amazed that there was anything left in the world for her to be afraid of.

*

In Terenten my father was stung by a wasp and suffered such a severe allergic reaction that he couldn't get out of bed for twenty-four hours. The knowledge that a second sting could be dangerous and possibly even fatal did not stop him from 'befriending' a wasp that visited him regularly in his office at the university. He had a habit of drinking juice in his office and this wasp came flying through the open window, attracted by the sugar. My father calmly watched as it drank from his glass and then flew away again. He wondered: was it always the same wasp, that had learned with insect intelligence about the open window and the juice, or was it merely by chance that different wasps, passing by on different days, happened to find the same opening? In order to resolve this question, he borrowed some red nail polish from a secretary, and very carefully, one day while the wasp was drinking its fill, painted a tiny red spot on its abdomen. And yes, it was always the same wasp that came to drink.

There came a succession of holidays when the office windows would remain closed for an entire week. This raised a new, intriguing question. Did wasps have long-term memory? Would the wasp have forgotten?

On Monday when my father returned to work, he opened his window and there it was, his wasp, marked in red, as if it had been waiting for him.

*

Each summer vacation took us a little further south. We rented other people's houses. One year someone gave my parents the address of a house in the Mugello valley just north of Florence. All the other places we'd been were forgotten in the beauty of the Mugello. My mother wrote in her diary about the olive groves, the cypresses, the white oxen ploughing the fields; the local peasants who were so courteous, tactful, open and genuine; the house we stayed in, built of golden sandstone, with red clay tile floors and whitewashed walls; the wealth of insects, lizards, frogs and bats; even the food which tasted so much better than at home: *mortadella, pecorino, toscanello,* melons, peaches, squash blossoms; only the bread she had a hard time getting used to.

I was thirteen, my brother Martin was nine. I fell in love with the gardener's son, Gabriele.

It turned out there were more houses where this one came from. Tenant farmers were abandoning their homes in large numbers, driven to find work in cities by the old *mezzadria*

74

system, which forced them to give half of their yield to the landowner. We went around looking at the empty crumbling buildings: doorways, arches, roofs partially caved in, windows shuttered. I remember going off on my own to explore, tiptoeing from one silent room to another with a feeling of almost unbearable suspense. In some cases it seemed as if the inhabitants had only just left, as if you could still hear the echoes of their voices. Other houses were already completely overgrown with brambles.

One house stood out. Its name was Collina. It had a simple rectangular shape and it stood on top of a hill looking down over the whole valley. You could see all the way to the Apennines in the distance. Ten years ago, there had been four families living in as many rooms; at the end it had been used by the shepherd, who had left his racks for drying cheeses in a room that was painted just exactly the blue of the cornflowers that grew around the house. The landowner who was selling it lived in a big villa at the bottom of his estate. He was a Marchese and his wife was related to Mussolini.

My parents discussed buying Collina. My father felt frightened of the idea of ownership, of the permanency and loss of freedom it implied. 'To own a little piece of earth,' I heard him say, trying to persuade himself, 'to be rooted to the planet.' But Collina had nothing to do with settling down: it was half a ruin. Both of them were nervous. They had never spent so much money before.

After our vacation was over they made another trip down by train to look again, by themselves. It was on the way back, in the hot, stuffy train compartment, that they decided. It seemed such a crazy, giddy thing to do that I imagine at that moment they looked very young. It was like acquiring a new dream of happiness together.

11

THE FIRST GLIMPSE OF Collina is from the narrow asphalt road that winds from the little town of Pontecchio out into the countryside. 'There it is!' my father shouts excitedly, swerving the car. 'Where? Where?' It is still only a tiny sand-coloured shape up in the hills, and you can only see it for a brief moment; but it is unmistakably recognizable because of the two outbuildings, the bake house and the chicken house, clustered near it. A little later we turn right at the Marchese's villa, off the asphalt and onto a stone and dirt path that winds steadily upward. Through some woods, past some deserted farm houses, then Beppe's farm, Giorgio's farm; another stretch of woods and suddenly, emerging, there it is again, Collina, much closer now, and how beautiful! It stands, golden in the late afternoon sun, beckoning to us, only an olive grove between us and it.

The road, ascending, has gotten steadily worse. Rainwater has dug deep ruts between jutting ridges of stone. The piece leading up to the house is the worst of all. We stop at the bottom of the hill. 'Do you think we can make it?' my father asks. 'How much weight do we have in the car?'

We invariably have a lot; in any case it is a rhetorical

question, since my father has packed the car himself. 'Oh, not that much,' my mother says.

'Maybe if the children got out . . . Well, OK, why don't we try it like this. If I get enough speed up, maybe I can do it.'

The hill has to be taken with just the right amount of speed. Too little and we'll lose momentum, get stuck. Too much and we may – as happened to a friend who visited us one time – overshoot the curve and end up in an olive tree. At the end of our long journey there is always this last little adventure.

We grip our seats as my father begins the dangerous ascent in first gear. Stones fly up against the bottom of the car, shoot out on either side, roll away under spinning tyres as we veer rapidly left and right in avoidance of ruts or large rocks. When we arrive at the top we gasp with relief: we made it!

*

The first year we came to stay, the Marchese's wife gave us as a house-warming present a little portable gas cooking stove, and the Marchese sold us a *damigiana* of the estate's red wine. While he stood smiling at our amazement (we had never seen such a large bottle before), his assistant lifted it from a wheelbarrow into the back seat of the car. We drove it up the mountain. My father wrestled with it, heaved it out of the car and set it down on the ground, where it broke on a piece of jagged rock. In less than a minute he watched forty litres of wine sink without a trace into the earth. When the Marchese heard of this disaster, he gave us another, smaller bottle as consolation.

It was early summer and the air was filled with the heavy fragrance of Scotch broom. The dry, hot noons were silent and the cool nights were tremulous with cicadas. But the evenings were best, long drawn-out, modulating slowly from warm gold to cool pink to darkness. There was a bit of flat ground just outside the kitchen door that became our 'terrace': here we ate our dinners and watched the spectacle of the sun as a great red fluid ball sliding out of sight behind the mountains. When it was over, when the last sliver of it was gone, we stayed to count the number of mountain ranges that could be distinguished in the distance, up to eight or nine silhouettes one behind the other, in ever-lightening shades of soft purple-grey. You could hear dogs barking in the valley and, very faintly, the music from the dance hall in the village.

A few days into our stay there was a thunderstorm; I remember being awakened in the middle of the night by a furious cracking right above the house. I heard rain pounding down on the roof and then, distinct from that, a high splashing sound as of a fountain. My mother appeared in her long white flannel nightgown carrying a candle. The electricity was out, and the roof was leaking.

She gave us each a candle and then we flitted about in the darkness, looking for leaks. In some places the water was merely dripping down, but in others it was gushing in through large holes. We moved furniture, distributed buckets and cooking pots underneath the leaks. Each time we thought we had found them all, we would stop, hush, and listen: and in between the peals of thunder, a small *plink, plink* would inform us of another leak we had missed, or a new one that had been created by some overflow or alternate channelling of the water between the clay roof tiles. The roof was like a sieve.

*

My mother collected things for Collina. Throughout the year, at second-hand shops and sales, she accumulated all the items that are needed in a household: dishes, cups, coffee pots, colanders, candles, sheets, towels, towel racks, hot-water bottles, tablecloths, spice jars, sugar bowls, wooden spoons, whisks, bread knives, fruit knives (a complete set of them, with bamboo handles), crème caramel moulds, frying pans, waste-paper baskets, down comforters, bedspreads, bedside lamps. Each trip we loaded a few more of her boxes into the car and she, single-handedly almost, transformed the empty house into a cosy home. Every morning of our vacation, she would work at restoring some piece of furniture that we had picked up, furiously scraping away at old paint, painstakingly scratching it out of crevices and articulations; then came other treatments, sanding and staining, and the final step was a coat of *Xyladecor*, brought down in large cans from Germany. My mother swore by *Xyladecor*. When we stood around admiring the final product, a table or *madia* that had been transformed from a piece of junk into a thing of beauty, she would express her gratitude to this miracle varnish, as if it had done all the work for her.

In the afternoons she sometimes took a nap, something she was able to do only in Collina; at home she was too restless and didn't have the necessary peace of mind. She said that it helped her go to sleep when I practised my flute in the adjacent room.

Every Easter and summer vacation from then on we worked on the house. We used to imagine Collina as it would be once it was 'all fixed up'. We thought of the *stalla* as the 'library' while it was still filled with manure. My father and I together loaded up seventeen wheelbarrows of manure and carted them twenty yards away from the house to a place where the hillside fell off somewhat precipitously, and dumped them over the edge. It is my father who remembers exactly the number of wheelbarrow trips that it took. What we didn't realize was that with all that manure we were fertilizing the brambles, the brambles that lay in wait, ready to choke the life out of a house that was neglected. After this, my father and I spent a certain amount of time each summer trying to fight back the brambles. My father was fanatical about it. We struck at them with sickles and scythes borrowed from our neighbour, Gino, and then we went after the roots with the *zappa*. This was one of the first good Italian words I learned – the hoe. Gino's *zappa* looked medieval, with a shaft polished through use but still resembling a tree bough, and a heavy hand-forged blade. Gino showed me how to use it, and then stood smiling and chuckling to himself as he watched me struggle with it.

The roots of brambles, we discovered, travel on and on underground. There was no way one could hope to simply pull them out.

12

THERE IS A PHOTOGRAPH of me when I was about fifteen, leaning against the railing of a boat on some outing of which I have no memory. My hair was cut in a short, tomboyish style and I was wearing a horrible trouser suit made out of carrot-coloured denim, bell-bottoms and a matching short jacket. I am appalled that I could ever have worn such a thing. Looking at the picture, I fixate on the impossible cut of this suit and its strident yellow-orange colour; I revel in a perverse joy of disgust over it. I want to avoid for as long as possible recognizing myself in that withdrawn pale-faced girl, her suspicious sideways glance at the camera.

I was often sick. I had a sore throat so frequently that my mother didn't bother any more to take me to the doctor. She simply shone a flashlight into it – I was expert at opening my gullet wide so that no tongue depressor was needed – and if it was inflamed, she prescribed me a ten-day regimen of penicillin from a never-ending supply which she kept in the medicine cabinet. Many years later I found out that she got this supply from a friend who was a horse veterinarian. 'Penicillin is penicillin,' my mother said. She would set up a special bedside table and on it she would put a pitcher of juice or water, a glass, and a timer. Before leaving for work, she admonished me to drink a glass of fluid at regular intervals.

I loved being sick. The feeling of well-being, the utter relief at not having to go to school, was so great as to overshadow any physical discomfort. When my parents had said goodbye and I heard the front door close behind them, I knew that I was really free. I gathered all my books around me and spent the happiest hours in the silence of our apartment.

One winter, when I was signed up for a skiing course on Sundays that I dreaded, I found that I could make myself sick. That winter, I had tonsillitis every other week. I only had to shower and wash my hair and then open the bathroom window wide to let in the cold winter air, and sit there for ten minutes or so without drying myself. It was that easy.

At sixteen I began seeing dermatologists. The first one, an old man, told me to go skiing and give up chocolate. The next had me eating raw yeast. It came in three-centimetre cubes at the grocery shop, a greyish paste like modelling clay. I kept it in the refrigerator near the eggs, and three times a day I'd break off little pieces and mould them into balls like 'pills', which I popped into my mouth with one hand while holding my nose with the other. Every evening I put on goggles and sat for ten minutes in front of a UV-lamp (the next best thing to skiing) which we set up on my mother's desk in the study; it put a funny taste into my mouth. A new doctor prescribed a lotion that I was to wear at night. It had to be specially mixed for me at the pharmacy, they gave me a brown glass jar labelled by hand, and when I opened it at home it turned out to be a thick, smooth, chalky-pink liquid. This was my favourite medicine. It was like the clown paint we used at carnival time, it made a mask on my face with holes for my eyes, nostrils and lips, which looked raw and sickly by contrast; and it came off on my pillow at night.

My father told me that when he was my age, his acne was much, much worse than mine – until he was given a radical cure. His entire facial skin was burnt off, his face was literally made to peel off in strips. After that the problem was gone.

Now, many years later, I learn that my father too had sore throats as a child. The doctor told him he was a *Schleimhaut-schwächling*: a mucous membrane weakling. While my tonsillitis got me out of skiing and out of school on certain crucial days, my father's got him excused from the Hitler Youth, which he hated, which meant having to march outdoors even in cold and rainy weather; or long, boring afternoons in which the leaders showed off in front of the younger boys by riding their motor-cycles round and round a field.

It was my father's job to type out notices for the next gathering. Since there were no xerox machines, he typed the same notice again and again on his little manual typewriter. At the bottom of each he had to type the words, ATTENDANCE IS MANDATORY! Then he delivered them to each boy's house on his bicycle.

He began making incendiary remarks at the dinner table, such as, 'The Nazis make me sick.' He could not have been more pleased by the reaction this produced: shocked silence, an exchange of grave looks. My grandmother's hand went over her mouth. *Um Gottes Willen!* At school he pushed his daring a little further, saying, offhand, about one of the teachers, 'The only reason he was promoted is because he's a Nazi.' My father had an ally in the elderly doctor whom he went to see because of his sore throats. The doctor used to say, and he used to probe my father as to the degree of devotion to Nazism among his classmates. He lent him books about amoebae and talked to him about science.

One evening, word went round that 'something's going on at the Prinz villa.' The Prinz family were Jews; they owned one of the fanciest clothing stores in town. The boys all went to see what was going on. My father remembers standing and watching as two SS stormtroopers tried to kick in the front door, failed, then decided it wasn't fun any more and they might as well go and have some beers instead.

In the end, it was a protracted infection under his thumb nail that liberated my father from the Hitler Youth exercises once and for all.

This puts my father's story about the letter he wrote to the *Jungstammführer* in a new light. It occurs to me that perhaps that letter wasn't, after all, a matter of calculated daring, the way he portrays it now, so much as a desperate attempt to make his sickliness work for him one more time.

*   *   *

It was spring or early summer. I was eighteen. My class was preparing for the final *Abitur* examinations, the end of our nine years in *Gymnasium*. We did not have school as usual, instead we were supposed to spend all our time studying at home. The weather was warm and sunny. In the morning I drank coffee and studied on our back balcony, facing east, and in the afternoon I sat on the front one, bathed in the warm sun, shielded from the street and the voices of playing children by the white and red geraniums that my mother had growing in her balcony pots. Sometimes groups of us studied together. Despite the pressure of the looming exams, there was at the same time a feeling of release and vacation, like a delicious foretaste of the freedom that awaited us after graduation. I couldn't remember any other spring and early summer of my life being so beautiful as this one was; or perhaps I'd just never experienced the beauty of the season more keenly.

Within my class, too, something strange was happening. A sort of movement and percolation had started; old and fast friendships had loosened and new ones formed. It had to do with the knowledge that this period in our lives was about to end, that in a few months we'd all be going off in different directions. For my part, since I had decided to go to college in America, I knew I wouldn't see many of my classmates ever again.

It was an intense time, nostalgia mixing with anticipation. Even the smallest things, like riding my bike on a foggy morning, could fill me with a sudden fierce happiness that seemed at the same time a wish for the future.

It was from this vantage, the consciousness of being about to embark on my life, that I suddenly perceived my father at a great distance, at the other end of it all, having stumbled, perhaps failed.

13

THE KNOWLEDGE that something was very wrong with my father must have filtered into my mind gradually. I think it had been there for a while before I put it together, brought it into my consciousness.

Something bad had happened to him. My mother told me about it. A series of experiments had pointed to an important discovery. Perhaps my father believed that this was the discovery of his lifetime, proving correct a certain theory he had advanced, that would revolutionize the understanding of the immune system. In his hopeful excitement and optimism, he presented the results at a conference in Paris before they had been confirmed by control experiments. That was going against the rules; it was something my father had never done before. But the results were only a week or two away from being confirmed, and this conference, filled with eminent scientists from around the world, was the ideal opportunity to present them.

My mother said that my father was more than usually nervous as he spoke. He had drunk something beforehand to summon up courage; his voice was hoarse and his hands were shaking.

When he returned from the conference, he found within

days that the results had been based on a mistake: some test tubes had been switched, mislabelled by a technician. He would have to retract his paper.

*

My parents tried to keep their problems hidden from my brother and me. When they quarrelled, they waited until after we'd gone to bed to confront each other. In the past I used to lie awake when they went out at night, worrying that something could happen to them on their way home. Now it was a different fear that kept me awake, the fear of suppressed resentment between them. I listened intently to their conversations, certain that at the next moment it must break out. When they did argue, I felt it was not the result of a moment's exasperation or anger, but an outburst of something that had long been swelling underneath the surface.

One night I was lying in bed and heard their voices, and I strained to hear whether there was aggression in them. I couldn't make out what they were saying. I felt reassured, I was already half persuaded that everything was OK. And then I heard my mother say in a loud whisper, 'I have problems too, and nobody cares about them, *nobody* . . .' A door was shut noisily.

I lay there completely motionless. I wanted to go and tell her, 'I do, I care . . .' But of course that was not what she needed.

I ached with love for my mother. If only I could help her more! It was true that my father had changed. He had begun to drink red wine by himself in the evenings. It made him sentimental and then he pitied himself. I could see that he kept drawing understanding and support from my mother, without giving her anything in return. She had to bear all of our burdens.

After they had both gone to bed I got up again: I couldn't sleep. I went to the kitchen and warmed up some milk; I added honey and cinnamon and cloves. I drank it sitting at the long, empty dining-room table. In the silence, the dark doorways on all sides of me seemed menacing, as if the rooms behind them had turned into hostile, unfamiliar places. I still kept on listening intently, even though now there was nothing to hear.

After a while I was too tired to think anything. I stared absent-mindedly at the traces of spice that had remained at the bottom of my cup, and then I began to move them around with the trickle of milk that was left, tilting the cup first to one side and then the other. It was like telling fortunes with tea leaves. I used my spoon to scrape and shove, altering the design.

*

My father had been complaining that he did not feel well. At last he gave in to my mother's entreaties and made an appointment for a physical check-up. He went to see Dr Uhland, the husband of one of his laboratory associates.

The diagnosis was a light case of hepatitis – nothing too serious, but it called for rest and observation. My father had to stay in the hospital for a week or so. Without a doubt, my father said, he must have contracted the hepatitis when he ate so many raw mussels in Paris after the conference. There was a lot of talk about hepatitis A and B, though I don't remember which it was that he had.

My mother decided that this was the perfect occasion for my father to give up smoking. Here it was, a week without any stress or obligations, and certainly smoking must be forbidden in the hospital rooms. She hoped that the strictness of the nurses in enforcing this regulation would achieve what she in all her married years had failed to do.

My mother had always hated my father's smoking. She hated the smell and the messiness of pipe ashes. It was because of these ashes that we had kept the same ugly carpet all these years – it was no use getting a new one, she would say, the corners of her mouth bitterly set, as long as my father kept smoking his pipes. Of course she was worried about the consequences for his health. But mostly she hated the principle of it. She called it 'a filthy habit'.

My father's smoking was the scapegoat on which, over the years, all my mother's dissatisfactions with her marriage came to be concentrated. For a while she had tried banning his pipes from our apartment, insisting that he smoke only on the balcony. Then again there were periods when she ignored it, resigned herself to it. Her hatred of it cropped up periodically, like a recurrent rash. I think she had brought herself to believe that if only she could win this battle, all would be well again with him and between them.

Every day that my father was in the hospital, my mother visited him there, smug in the knowledge that she had all his pipes at home where he couldn't reach them.

On the last day before he was to come back home, she entered his room and saw him hastily slip something under the covers. A pipe! The smell that hovered round his bed was unmistakable. My mother left the hospital abruptly, in a cold fury.

That evening, she did not call him as usual. I asked her when he was coming home and she replied, without looking up from her reading, that she didn't know and didn't care.

'I have nothing to say to him.'

Tearfully, I begged her to call him up; she refused. It became abundantly clear to me that we were not going to prepare any welcome-home festivities.

I spent the evening cutting and pasting letters out of coloured paper, making a sign that read 'Welcome Home'. This childish activity soothed me. I felt a sense of panic, a dread of something too large and serious for crying. I got out my old box of crayons that I had not used in many years, and started decorating the sign with flowers − red daisies with yellow centres, tulips with overlapping petals, green undulating vines with pointed leaves growing out of them. I kept making the sign more and more elaborate, working away after everyone else had gone to bed, as if I were trying with tiny patient stitches to mend the enormous rent that had appeared in the fabric of our family life.

My father came home the next afternoon. Of course he thanked me for the welcome-home sign. At the dinner table he asked, addressing himself to no one in particular, 'Where are all my pipes?' My mother answered: 'I threw them away the day after you went to the hospital.'

Of course this was untrue; she would not have thrown them away until the previous day, when she was so angry. I felt sure, though, that she hadn't thrown them away at all, but had merely hidden them.

A long silence followed my mother's words.

'I wondered whether you would do such a thing,' my father said slowly. 'But I thought, no, she wouldn't go that far. That would be too much...'

I went into my room and locked the door and started playing my flute very loudly, to drown out all thought of them.

*

My father took some time off from work. Things quieted down again. There was an understanding that he was making an effort to pull himself together, by resting and recuperating. Perhaps my parents had had it out and reached some kind of reconciliation. There was the idea of a fresh start, with promises given on both sides. Something like this is necessary to understand the effect it had on me when I discovered one afternoon that my father drank on the sly.

I remember going down the cellar stairs in a lackadaisical way. I was pretending to myself that I was really just going to get something from the pantry. I don't know what I expected to find. I don't believe I was thinking anything at all; I was in a sort of trance of purposefulness. It didn't take long. I came almost immediately upon those bottles of *Schnaps*, and I knew right away that I had found what I was looking for.

14

'HONEYMOON, ETC.' I've found the old 8mm movie reel in my mother's storage closet, with the title printed in her neat hand on the side of the aluminium case. I've taken it secretly and had it converted to video.

The picture opens with a view of a white balloon, floating aside to reveal a squad of men identically dressed, executing synchronized, half-dancing steps to the left and to the right. Rose Parade, 1957: probably the first footage taken with the newly bought camera. A Chinese pagoda comes into view, with a two-tiered roof, corners pulled airily up. Everything made of roses. There follows a gigantic roast chicken, resting on a bed of potatoes – all roses; then an elephant, a rocket, a butterfly moving its wings.

The floats pull out of sight slowly, cumbersomely, with the heaviness of truck tyres and gasoline engines labouring beneath the flowers. Slim-waisted ladies with bare shoulders and long white gloves wave to the crowd like fairies from lily pads. There are majorettes kicking up their legs; and another band of musicians, playing tubas with huge, outrageous mouths made of transparent red plastic, the whole row of them turning and wagging in unison. They look ludicrous and pathetic now, without their joyous noise, completely silent but for the low buzz of the video machine as it transports the film. The colours, too, are all faded. All those millions of roses faded to dim, wan colours like old sugar paper.

I feel an almost painful suspense in watching these beginning sequences. My parents' presence is only implied as the eyes that are seeing all this world. Once my father let the camera slip, he dropped it and it swung for a moment from the strap around his neck. It caught a piece of fabric close-up, whitish, perhaps plaid, you can't tell for sure. Was that my mother's dress? It's not that this footage of the Rose Parade is interesting in itself; in fact it's excruciatingly boring. All the interest was in the moment, the here-and-now, in their watching it together, the intimate happiness of experiencing it together, watching that jumpy, silly parade pass by. That was what my father was trying to capture on his camera. And so I am watching this thing with the faded colours as if it were some kind of riddle or coded message, trying, by following everything that those eyes were following, to see with those eyes, to get a glimpse behind them.

I have to be patient.

We are tourists in San Francisco now. In a restaurant high above the city, we are panning across the picture windows, taking in a magnificent view over the bay and into the hills beyond. It is a beginner's shot: the view turns out to be too distant to be interesting. Instead, though, the people sitting in front of the windows, appearing as black silhouettes, are sharply defined and mysterious, as in the hard and cold, enigmatic world of a spy thriller.

Down by the water, a Chinese family is fishing from a pier: men, women in scarves, a few toddlers. They are fishing for their dinner in the shadow of a splendid two-masted sailing ship, and seem as oblivious to its anachronistic beauty as if it were a rock or a mountain. A little way off, two men lean on a wooden railing, talking as they look at the water. They are wearing sunglasses, and hats pulled down into their faces. They are skinny, slick, cruel-looking, like small-time gangsters, doing the dirty work of those silhouette men high above in the restaurant.

Three old Italian men sit peacefully on their bench, gossiping. A boy fishes from a small rowing boat, his line vertically piercing the oily-calm surface of the water. A large fishing boat, blue and white, with the name *Martha* clearly legible on the prow, is returning to harbour. We watch the bustle of the crew as they fasten it, prepare to bring their haul ashore. The youngest fisherman lets his water-repellent trousers slip down negligently, as if by accident: it's a fleeting, alluring moment, that almost went unnoticed.

Since having the reel converted to video I have watched it, not just once or twice, but perhaps as many as six times. And still there are moments like this that I hadn't seen before.

At times it becomes almost unbearable: I have such a burning curiosity for everything *except* this little segment that the camera happens to show. The only reason I keep watching it is that it allows me to infer, or not even to infer but at least to guess, to daydream about all the things that were not in the viewfinder.

*

On the way back, driving through the desert, they had a punctured tyre. My father shot a close-up of the tyre sitting very flatly on the yellow desert ground, hooded by the enormous blue fender of the '53 Buick he had recently bought. In the background you can see cars whizzing by on the road and a red STOP sign, as a serendipitous emblem of their predicament. I can just imagine the pride he must have felt over this shot, so economical, telling an entire story with only a few elements.

No choice but to get out the tools and change the tyre. 'Let's film it,' he must have said. 'It's an adventure.' And I imagine him showing my mother how to use the camera. 'It's easy. Just hold it like this, and press this button. You will probably have to get down a little . . .'

She kneeled and filmed him as he pumped the jack up and down, looking at her the whole while, grinning widely as if it were a big joke. He must have been so different from the other men she knew, for whom a tyre change would have been a matter of seriousness and self-importance, a chance to display their mechanical competence. With him it was ironic, as if he were showing off and at the same time laughing at himself for showing off. He knew perfectly well how to change a tyre, but it looked odd on him, as if he were trying on someone else's clothes.

Nothing was ever merely, drearily 'real' with my father: it was fascinating, or strange, or an adventure.

Here is my mother, wheeling the new tyre round to where it is needed. At the same time, a very beautiful, sleek Dalmatian has appeared out of nowhere to keep them company. It strolls casually into the scene, sniffs somewhat embarrassingly, then ambles on, inspecting the car. Where did it come from? No houses for miles around: and yet it looks well-kept and elegant, striking in its black and white pattern, and as nonchalant as if it were simply paying a polite social visit. It is unexplained, mysterious.

Afterwards: my father sitting on the ground, leaning against the side of the car with its new tyre, the weary mechanic. He takes a swig from a bottle – it looks like motor oil, perhaps cold coffee – and passes the back of his hand in an exaggerated motion over his mouth. 'Aaah!' End of the episode.

But wait. My mother, already in the car, thinking they are about to leave, is putting on lipstick in the rear-view mirror. He catches her at it. I have to spool back the tape to see it again. How was that? That smile that she flashed in his direction: it happened so quickly – there and gone. But even after spooling it back several times it is too fast for me to grasp. Insubstantial, evanescent, the kind of moment that wasn't meant to be caught on camera, much less described.

*

The scene has changed. My father is rowing a boat in some kind of a pond, in a park. It must be my mother again, sitting across from him, who is filming. His mouth is moving: he is speaking non-stop, trying to seem natural, trying to keep a straight face as he tugs at the oars. A grin cracks crookedly, is suppressed, then suddenly breaks loose into a wild, young laugh that I have never seen on him. The oars and camera are exchanged. There is my mother, dressed in white and blue, with pretty seashells around her neck, frowning with the effort, dimpling, looking over her shoulder to see where she is going. Her younger sister is sitting next to her, Marianne, in blue and white. 'Talk to each other,' my father says. 'Say something.' My mother looks at Marianne and speaks. Marianne looks embarrassed and uncomfortable, and says nothing. She doesn't want to be part of this. The camera leaves her in peace and dotes again on my mother. Her girlish beauty, the blond curls blown across her head by the breeze. It is her turn now to try and stay serious; but the laughter bursts out of her all the harder. It explodes!

When I come to this part I always feel like a voyeur. They

both seem so young. Their youngness seems younger than I ever was or anyone I know. They look newly hatched; as tender and fragile as seedlings just pushing their heads out of the soil. I feel that this movie is forbidden material. There is almost an indecency in my watching it now. It is something to be kept tightly locked away, forgotten, denied and suppressed. The present is difficult enough without holding before one's eyes what it was that has been ruined and taken away.

*

At the end of the reel is the jewel, a little sequence that starts with a view of a wedding cake, standing by itself on a pedestal in the grass by the side of a white house.

No one in sight.

But there, from behind a bush, as if by chance, appear the bride and groom, followed by a bevy of little ladies in pastel chiffon circle dresses. My grandmother, my aunt, and another woman whom I don't recognize, perhaps an aunt or a neighbour. My mother is dressed, by contrast, in a white suit of severe elegance, with an enormous collar enfolding her shoulders like a pair of wings.

'Ah! Look what we have found! A wedding cake!' they seem to say. 'Shall we cut it?' My father, the only male present, is wearing a loosely cut black suit; his hair has been oddly curled or moulded at the top of his head so that it won't fall forward. They cut, ceremoniously and awkwardly, his hand on top of hers. She feeds him a piece, then he her. 'Would you like some more?' – 'Oh, no, thank you, it tastes so awful.' This she says smiling brightly, mischievously, knowing that the camera can't hear.

Then there are some poses, group photos; whoever was holding the camera was inept, because half the time the heads are cut off. I wonder what my mother's family thought of this German who, merely for the sake of having some sort of action (it's a *moving picture*, after all), begins shaking everyone's hands, very formally, pumping them up and down. Then, clownishly, he takes his wife's hand and begins shaking it even more vigorously, and the two of them laugh as if it were an old joke between them. 'Germans always shake hands.' I know my grandmother, however affectionately she put her arm around him for the camera, objected to the marriage. She didn't want my mother to marry a foreigner.

The final scene shows the newly-weds in their car, embarking on their honeymoon, waving as they pull out of the picture. I was confused the first time I watched the movie. Why was it all in reverse, the honeymoon trip before the wedding?

Then I realized. The honeymoon trip ended in a terrible crash, a collision with a truck. My parents might have died, but for the old heavy Buick, with its huge blue bonnet, that enormous expanse of metal. The Buick saved their lives. To avoid this conclusion my father artfully cut the film so as to make a circle: when you reached the end it brought you back to the beginning. He used that simple story-telling trick by which time is prevented from going forward, and instead circles forever, biting its tail.

15

THE THINGS I'VE BEEN TOLD about the past, about the time before I was born, are too few to be fitted together properly. They are like archaeological fragments; I shift them around, trying to discern the shape of a deeper story.

The time after the war was hard, there was no food at all, everything was destroyed, the future inconceivable. My father always told us that he used to walk six kilometres to some relatives' farm where they would give him a rind of bacon or a couple of eggs. The irony of it, he pointed out: the caloric value of the food he was given was certainly less than what he expended in walking to this farm and back.

The letters from my grandfather had stopped coming. For a long time my grandmother waited, hoping with each release of prisoners from Russia that he would be among them. Very gradually, this hope diminished.

Standing in line for food stamps, my grandmother was abused by the villagers. She drew herself up, stood a little taller. She instilled in her children a consciousness of inner distinction, a sense of high caste brought low, nobility in rags. *We lost everything.* She worked for a while in a cottage industry, painting tin garden gnomes and knitting sweaters on a machine.

Life was topsy-turvy, crazy things seemed possible or even normal. American jazz was playing on all the phonographs, and cinemas were springing up like mushrooms. My grandmother conceived the following plan for herself and her family: by selling her engagement diamond she could start a small cinema of her own. She would sit behind a window selling tickets while my father, with his technical talents, could run the film projector. But my father did not want to run a projector.

In order to apply to my grandfather's bank for his pension, my grandmother had to officially declare him dead. She used the money from her diamond to rent a small apartment in the nearest town where my father and his sisters could finish school. Ten years later, my grandmother was still writing letters, trying to find her husband or at least to learn what had happened to him.

Somewhere during this time, there was the story of Onkel Hermann's inheritance. My grandfather's brother had gone to Chile in the twenties to make his fortune in curtain manufacturing. He hadn't been heard from until one day, some time after the end of the war, a letter arrived from Punta Arenas addressed to my grandfather. It was written in Spanish and my grandmother had to find someone who could translate it. It was the notification of Hermann's death. He had named my grandfather as his heir. My grandmother had the choice either to accept or decline the inheritance.

This was exciting news, as romantic as stumbling upon buried treasure. My father, now seventeen, was aflame with the idea that the money should be used to buy a car, a gleaming new Studebaker. But the letter did not disclose any specific sums, it made no reference to money at all. My grandmother grew suspicious. What if the inheritance consisted entirely of debts? In the end she decided, much to her children's disappointment, to refuse it.

Nevertheless, some months later they received a box in the mail, covered with Chilean stamps, battered and crushed and barely held together by string. When they opened the package they found it contained nothing more nor less than a black tuxedo in perfect condition.

Afterwards they learned, from an acquaintance of an acquaintance who had been in Punta Arenas, that Hermann and his wife had died in a widely publicized double suicide. His curtain factory had gone under long ago and had been followed by a series of other failed ventures. The two German immigrants were found in a hotel room. Hermann had shot first his wife and then himself with an ordinary pistol.

Years later, the tuxedo would come in handy. My father wore it when he received his doctorate. Later still, Erika took it apart at the seams and made herself a suit in which she celebrated her engagement.

*

My father finished school and began to study physics, then biology, in Tübingen. He was a *Studienstiftler*; the recipients of this fellowship lived in a special dormitory, it was considered a sort of genius club. My mother remembers my father telling an anecdote that had impressed him. Each student had to give a yearly progress report. Once a student wrote the following single sentence for his report: 'This year, I was so terribly in love that I did nothing at all.' The head of the group was delighted. He read it aloud, as epitomizing the *Studienstiftler* ethic of soaring above rules and requirements.

My father as the young 'genius': it's this era of his life that is the most difficult for me to contemplate. I find my thoughts shying away from it. I have some photos from his student years. In one he is posed in a laboratory, bending over a microscope, impossibly handsome. The high forehead pulls the face upward; between the combed back hair and the eyes there's a tautness as of a sail in the wind. The clear, light-coloured eyes seem suspended. Perhaps it's that I fear I myself would have found him irresistible, would have succumbed to his charm. His charisma, his great promise. How easily everything comes to him. There is a cheekiness about him in these photos, just a hint of an ironic grin in the corners of his mouth, as of someone who knows he can get away with things; who is not about to be caught in the nets that catch and entangle other people.

*

When my father departed for America, he left behind a fiancée, Dorothea, who had already felt herself as part of the family. He seems to have gone looking only forward, turning his back on what lay behind. When, perhaps a year or two later, he married my mother, he didn't even bother to let my grandmother know about it beforehand. He only told her afterwards, in a letter, when the deed was done.

My aunt Hannelore once explained to me, as an excuse for my father, that at that time going to America was not like it is now, when people fly back and forth and think nothing of it. Then, she said, people left and often didn't come back for years, if ever. It was a major voyage, a definitive departure.

A photo album begun in the year of my parents' marriage contains small black-and-white shots taken during my mother's first visit to Germany with my father. These pictures, group portraits with his family, amaze me. It's not even so much that I am looking for my mother in each of them as that she shines out as some creature who does not belong there. Cramped on dark sofas under heavy, glossy picture frames, surrounded by old relatives in black suits and gloomily patterned silks, amidst the ponderous festivity of champagne being poured to toast the recently wedded couple, my mother is radiantly beautiful. On some pictures she has a dreamy, faraway expression. On others she is all smiles, easily pleased and eager to please. Wearing a simple sleeveless white dress, she has a look of innocence, like a Sleeping Beauty just awakened from a thousand years' sleep.

She has come a long way from that small California ranch where she grew up. Her mother was a schoolteacher, her father a veterinarian who taught future farmers at the community college. They had a few cows; several acres of walnuts and, planted alongside the walnuts, every kind of fruit tree under the sun. Pears and apricots. White peaches, yellow peaches, red peaches. My mother remembers playing with her sister Marianne in the muddy rivulets created by the irrigation system. She saved up money for college by raising chickens; she couldn't stand the birds, their stupidity and murderous cruelty toward each other. Pictures I've seen show a shy, gangly girl in denim overalls with two thin blond plaits. My mother hated wearing the frilly dresses that my grandmother constantly sewed for her. She liked animals – with the exception of chickens. She ran about with a butterfly net, chloroforming her specimens in a glass jar and attaching them to a piece of cardboard with pins from her mother's sewing box. America entered the war when she was seven and she was not yet eleven when it ended. It was a distant thing.

Because my mother received full fellowships to college and graduate school, her chicken money went to pay off the substantial debts my father had accumulated before their marriage.

My father insists to this day that he owed his first job, in

Munich, to my mother: that he got it because the head of the institute liked her. My mother was allowed to finish the research for her doctorate in the same laboratory.

Munich in 1959 seemed to my mother a grey and joyless city. The people walked about with their eyes to the ground, unfriendly and mean-spirited. She says she was surprised how many things had not yet been rebuilt after the war, how much rubble still lay about. Part of the building they lived in had been bombed and the steps were still broken. My mother became pregnant with me. She suffered from morning sickness. One morning she had to take a train somewhere and along the way, the sickness began rising in her. She was able to suppress it just long enough to reach her destination and get off the train. In the waiting room of the station, she vomited into a garbage can. While she was still recovering, a policeman approached her. She thought he was going to offer assistance. Instead he said: 'That will be ten marks for defiling public property.'

In the photos I am looking at now my mother does not appear unhappy or uncomfortable, only perhaps slightly bemused at the accident that has set her down in this particular place.

16

THE DAY I FOUND the bottles that my father had hidden in our cellar, I remember walking straight out of the house and down the street. It was a sunny day, some time in the afternoon. I wanted to run, to run away; but there was nowhere for me to run, so I walked. I was conscious of the swinging of my arms as being a false, unnatural movement. It seemed that, although the world looked unchanged, its gravity had somehow been altered, making it impossible for me to walk naturally.

On the surface our life continued the same as usual. I went to school, came home to Frau Blume's lunches, practised my piano and flute. But I knew that everything now was completely different. We were suspended above an abyss, waiting to fall.

My father seemed to have lost something essential, some basic ingredient without which it wasn't possible to live. Everything bored him. It was as if a vast cold emptiness were sucking him in. His emptiness spread through the apartment and began to swallow everything up. It froze my thoughts, drew the warmth out of my room where I was studying for my exams, made the pages of my book look blank.

He made frequent and prolonged visits to the toilet where he leafed through old *Bunte* or *Spiegel* magazines and talked to himself in a rumbling voice. In that tiny cubicle of a room, which contained nothing but the toilet, a small sink and a shelf piled with magazines, isolated from the world by the high-pitched whirr and drone of the ventilator, he seemed to find some kind of ease. He escaped into fantasized or remembered situations. It was usually impossible to understand what he was saying but sometimes the cadence seemed to indicate a dialogue. He would repeat phrases over and over again. Even when I could understand a sequence of words, they were incomprehensible, taken out of context. Often he laughed, as if he were telling himself jokes. Despite the ventilator, the room smelt for hours afterwards of stale tobacco smoke.

I felt that my father was terribly alone. None of us could reach him. As far as I knew, he had no friends.

Sometimes he came into the study while I was practising the piano. While I played, he would potter around behind my back, mumbling to himself, casually picking up things on his messy desk as if searching for something. Finally, after this show of desultoriness, when he thought he had lulled me into forgetting about his presence, he would open the cabinet containing the chemicals he used to restore and clean his antique globes. My father hadn't cleaned his globes in a long time. I knew that he kept there a jar of clear alcohol which he drank. I forced myself to keep on playing: I was afraid of his noticing that I had noticed something.

I thought that there was very little separating my father from the drunks at the train station, those frighteningly degraded, rawly exposed beings who nestled in the warm atmosphere around sausage and beer stands.

I became intent on not letting anything my father did escape me. I acquired sharp hearing: I was avid for this knowledge that hurt me. From behind the closed door of my room where

I sat reading, I could hear, through the flight of rooms of our apartment, through the front door, down the stairs to the basement, and there down another long hallway, the tiny sound of the key turning in the lock of our cellar room. It was not so much that the sound travelled all this distance to reach me, as that my hearing travelled, reaching to find the sound.

I tried to imagine the worst that could happen to us. I worried what would happen when my mother found out about my father's drinking; that she might somehow have a breakdown, leaving me to cope with him. I was vague on what it meant to 'have a breakdown'; but this idea of being left without a buffer between myself and my father was without question the most frightening prospect of all.

I decided one day to ask my father to go for a walk with me, and talk to him openly, 'man to man'. I see us now, walking after dinner, the usual route toward the lake. My father could not be more unlike those drunks at the train station. He seems touched by my concern. He can of course see the courage it has cost me to approach him openly like this. He is affectionate, fatherly, but mostly flattered by the quasi-heroic role in which he feels cast by my seriousness. He is utterly insincere in his promises to 'do better'. He prefers to feel himself an anti-hero, pulled down into the depths by forces irresistible, stronger than himself. In order to impress me even more, he says in a tortured voice (I picture him at this moment grasping his forehead; but I may be inventing this histrionic gesture), 'And you don't even know the worst of it yet.'

The 'you' was plural, meant to include my mother. I'd been saying we couldn't allow her to find out about those bottles in the basement. It was a sort of pact I'd offered him: I wouldn't tell her about my discovery, if he pulled himself together and stopped drinking.

'What do you mean?'

'I can't tell you.'

I was insulted, indignant: the least I deserved now was to be treated as an adult. I also felt that, under the terms of our pact, he owed me the complete truth.

'You're having an affair?' The words came out sarcastically, contemptuously, although I was choked with fear.

He looked at me for a moment, then shook his head. 'No, no. I can't tell you. I just can't.'

Back home again, I was confused. On the surface our talk seemed to have gone well; but there was a sense of anticlimax, as if the whole thing had been somehow not real.

* * *

The very thing that I feared most was happening. My mother was going away for a month to visit her family in California. She hadn't seen them in a couple of years. She told me she thought it might be good for my father if she went away for a while.

Her absence brought about a curious intensification of my relationship with my father. In the evenings when he came home from the laboratory, we were often alone together. My brother was out with his friends, or shut up in his room. I felt that I couldn't stay in my room, I had to sit in the living room with my father to keep him company, filling the space that my mother had left.

From the moment of my mother's departure, I waged a constant struggle against the emptiness that was threatening my father. I had to somehow fill this emptiness with my own person. I sat in my mother's chair, pretending to be absorbed in a book. I wanted him to follow my example, and immerse himself in something. I put on records – Schubert, his favourite – and urged him to try reading *The Brothers Karamazov*, which I had recently finished. I really believed that if only he paid attention to the music or a book, he could be saved, at least for the moment.

And all the time, I watched him. I felt like a nurse keeping vigil over a patient in a crisis of illness, whose life depended on staying awake. I was focused, concentrated in a keen awareness of my father's state of mind. I read every sign, every move that he made. With pretended nonchalance I would address some casual remark or question to him at what I perceived to be crucial moments. Or better, because it forced him to become involved, I would ask him for help or advice with something. I watched him with the tension of a cat ready to spring. Like some kind of animal, I was in a state of heightened instincts, barely conscious, without volition, dominated by this watchfulness. I registered the changes in my father – the clutching at some idea or hope, the lapsing back into vacant despondency – as precisely as if they had occurred within myself.

What irony when, one evening when we had been sitting together like this, he turned to me and said, in a friendly way: 'You don't quite know what to do with yourself today, am I right?'

My father's depression terrified me all the more because I had a sense that the same thing could easily happen to me. I wrote in my journal, with a furiously clenched hand that deformed my writing: 'I am just like him. I am exactly like him. I am exactly the same.' I flayed myself with this recognition.

*

Every day I waited in fear for the moment when my father, coming home from the laboratory, would unlock the door and

I would see at a glance if he was drunk. The first sign would be that his eyes were teary, the irises seeming to spill over as a chalky, pale blue fluid. His voice would be deep and his speech slow and ponderous. He would repeat the same statements over and over again.

When he was drunk I loathed him, I hated him with all my heart. But when, instead, my anxiety proved unfounded and he came home sober, I was so relieved that I loved him ten times as much, humbly and gratefully because he had resisted the temptation. The worst were the times when I couldn't be sure. Then I felt at the same time guilty because I might be suspecting him wrongly, and betrayed, because he might be deceiving me into thinking him sober.

One Saturday, while my mother was still away, I'd invited Monika and her brother Peter for lunch. Already in the morning of that day, my father's eyes were moist and his speech was hampered as if he had difficulty moving his tongue.

I noticed that he kept going into the study, and coming out with something hidden in his hand.

I confronted him. I don't remember exactly the words I used:

'You're drunk. You've been drinking. You keep it in the cabinet with your chemicals. I know . . .'

He categorically denied it, and since I had no proof, I had to accept his word so as not to accuse him of lying. I could not bring myself to accuse my father of lying. I even apologized for falsely suspecting him.

A little later, when I had begun to prepare our lunch, he came and stood swaying in the kitchen door. He said I was SNEAKY.

'Like a big SPIDER,' he said, 'sitting in the corner WATCHING and waiting to POUNCE on people.'

His voice was hoarse. Drunkenness helped him to a spectacular way of speaking, a kind of Strindbergian cold intensity that struck terror in me. It was too gothic, too theatrical, for our little low-ceilinged German apartment.

'I'm sorry,' I whimpered, pleading, hoping that would be the end of it.

But, as if he hadn't heard me at all, he went away and came back again: 'Just like a SPIDER. That's what you ARE . . .'

And again: 'You sit up there in your corner, in your WEB, WATCHING people . . .'

Part of me felt he was literally right: he had seen through me. Since I had previously felt myself as a kind of animal, it was easy to go an extra step and believe that I was really an ugly, hairy-legged, preying spider. For a moment I was horrified at this truth he had shown me about myself.

Finally he left the kitchen. I continued with my preparations. I silently began to cry, while cutting a tomato.

At lunch with my friends he sat at the head of the table, his eyes watering (he wiped at them occasionally with the back of his hand), making inane remarks, slowly pushing dripping forkfuls of salad into his mouth. I felt sick with shame. And I was consumed with hatred, because I knew that he had lied.

17

My mother has come back home and things have gone from bad to worse. We have never spoken about it. One evening she comes out of the kitchen and embraces me, saying, 'When will all this finally be over?' I pretend not to know what she is talking about. 'What do you mean?' She steps back, looks at me for a moment and then replies, evasively, 'Oh, all the uncertainty and problems.'

Sometimes I have to close myself off like this. I act cold and uncomprehending. I don't feel strong enough to have her confide in me.

Another day, dropping me off somewhere, she tells me in the car that she is worried about my father. He has no joy in life, she says, and their relationship isn't too good either. His helpless behaviour is forcing her into the role of 'mother and schoolteacher'. He resents her for treating him like a child; and she, for her part, wants someone to lean and depend on herself.

Again I stay silent, overwhelmed by confusing emotions. I want to be a source of strength to my mother. But her words grate on me, they're insulting, they seem to convey such a primitive, inadequate understanding. Her attempt to talk to me actually creates a separation between us, because it implies that I don't see what is happening, that I'm not suffering from it too.

We've gone so long without communicating that it's somehow too late: the reality has become too large and encompassing. For me there has come to be a kind of taboo around what is happening in our family. It's too terrible to be talked about, to be trivialized in conversation.

I wonder how fragile my mother is. She talks about the good friends she had in America and I am only beginning to understand how stranded and isolated she must feel here.

I am glad to be leaving for college. I feel guilty about this: how cowardly of me to run away and leave them here.

*

In her weekly letters to me at college, my mother never talks about my father. Her letters are always filled with trivial little details, and my letters to her are the same, and if I ever ask her about him, my questions are phrased in such a way that she knows I don't really want to know.

One day I receive a message that my mother has phoned and has asked me to call back. She has never called me at college before. I'm certain that a calamity has happened, that my father has committed suicide. A kind of hysterical anticipation grows in me with surprising quickness; I am on the verge of crying as I race down the library steps.

It never even occurs to me that my mother could be calling because it is my birthday.

*

I come home at Christmas, then again in the summer. I find everything exactly as it was before I left. I feel that I myself have changed completely; but here in our apartment the very air seems to be still the same air that I had breathed before leaving. The smells, the sounds are all the same, the dinner table conversation might have picked up from the day before or six months ago, it makes no difference.

Yet it's completely untrue that there are no changes: my brother has grown half a foot taller and my father's appearance has altered drastically. I stand and look at him one evening when he has fallen asleep on the sofa. He is sprawled out; his head has fallen back onto the cushions and his mouth hangs open. Until this point I have always thought of my father as being young, but now he looks old. He has sprouted a large, disfiguring belly, all the more grotesque because the rest of him is still thin. His skin looks unhealthy, reddish, yet as though not alive, and the pouches under his eyes have become more pronounced. But it is no single physical detail that makes him look decrepit so much as his entire posture – his hands limply at his sides, the despicable posture of someone who is not sleeping from tiredness, from hard work or lack of sleep, but from sheer emptiness.

I stare at him for a long time, forcing myself to take everything in, feeding my hatred as if I could become stronger through it.

*

My father becomes either cruel or sentimental when he is drunk. His cruelty is verbal: he'll run my brother down sarcastically or say things designed to cut my mother to the quick. Perhaps the sentimentality is worse. He'll seem to be begging for affection; tears frequently flood his eyes. It makes one recoil coldly and then feel guilty for rejecting him. With me he is more often sentimental than cruel. I hate being alone with him. He gazes at me blearily for long stretches of time, always wants to know what I am reading. Once he asks if he can read my diary.

Even in this state he retains a kind of power over me. At times when I would want to repulse him I find myself instead acting understanding and sympathetic. I hate myself for it afterwards.

There are intervals when he is sober again, when his old, humorous, intelligent self comes back. Then my defences break down, I can't remain aloof and hardened, as I would like to: I still love him, in spite of myself. It's a wasted love. It can't help him.

The worst is this feeling of abandonment that comes from seeing him transformed, the same and yet different. It is a form of betrayal, insidious because I am tricked again and again into forgiving it. He is two separate people; the sober one claims no responsibility, doesn't remember the drunk. I am left alone with my anger.

*

One day, crossing the Rhine on my bicycle, I happen to witness an accident. A motor boat is banging up against the concrete pillars that support the bridge; smoke is coming out of the boat, it is obviously out of control. There is no one steering – perhaps the driver has had a heart attack? – and I've arrived at the very moment where it has started smashing into the pillars. I get off my bicycle and watch, and a feeling of happy excitement fills me. I am at first shocked at registering this emotion in myself. Then I understand it: amidst the slow, continual catastrophe of our life, a descent so gradual that there is no end in sight, here at last is a real calamity, one that will shortly be over and come to rest in the destruction of the boat.

Sometimes I secretly think that the only way we could ever be happy again would be if my father died. I have fantasies of receiving the notification of an accident that has befallen him; of concealing my relief under a suitable show of sorrow.

*

My mother has to be strong, there is nothing that frightens me so much as the prospect of discovering the slightest sign of her strength cracking. This is the real reason why I discourage confidences between us. I am afraid of her showing weakness, afraid that if she gives in even a little bit she will crumble altogether. As long as she is forced to appear strong, for her children's sake, she will be strong.

But sometimes it is pure selfishness. I feel vexed if she tries to burden me with 'her problems': what kind of a *mother* is this?

*

I have fallen asleep; it must be a few hours later when I wake up with a feeling as if I'd been having nightmares, although I can't remember anything. The light in the hallway is still on, my mother and father are still up and about. What's going on? What's the matter? My chest tightens with fear and I jump up, run out into the hallway, follow the lights to the kitchen where I see my father in his pyjamas, bending down at a cabinet; from his hand dangles something terrible, the width of a finger and twice as long, yellow, jelly-like. Quickly he conceals it, I've only seen it for a split second.

'What's up?' I ask, trying to sound nonchalant.

'Nothing. Go back to bed, I'm going to bed now too.'

I go back to my room; my mother is standing in the bathroom, putting her hair up in pin curls. She has just showered and is wearing her pink summer nightgown. In the past I sometimes used to wake up late at night like this, to find the lights still on, one or the other of my parents just out of the shower; and I guessed that they had 'made love'. I had a vague notion of what this meant in any case, but in theirs I thought it must be particularly disgusting, since they had to clean themselves afterwards. I always felt resentful that they hadn't been more careful not to wake me up. On this occasion the idea springs into my mind that my father must have raped my mother.

I go back to bed filled with dread and misgiving; it really is like a nightmare, I can't make sense of anything any more. The yellow dangling thing – did I really see something or was it just a horrible hallucination?

*

Another night, as I lie tensely in bed, waiting for the lights in the hallway to go out, I suddenly think to myself: 'Look at it all from a greater distance, from an aeroplane perspective, think of the centuries of mankind, we are really just a couple of ants of no importance, like the millions of others who have lived and are now living; our problems are no more terrible than any others. Nothing is really terrible.'

I love flying. When I step onto the plane that will carry me to America, I feel I am shedding my life. Nothing matters any more: it is all stripped away up there in the sky. I love airports, the many possible destinations listed on the electronic display, the thousands, millions of strangers. I love being alone among them, just one more anonymous face. Sometimes I can barely contain my glee as I return the greeting of the stewardess who meets passengers in the narrow doorway of the aeroplane. I look attentively at the way the door is made and feel a smug certainty in thinking how hermetically it will be sealed in a little while. At take-off I lean forward and my own impatience becomes the force that causes the plane to gather speed. *'Faster, faster, faster,'* I pray. I savour every aspect of the journey. Even the cellophane-wrapped dinners taste like divine morsels to me, because they are eaten above the clouds.

It's not just that I am leaving my family behind: I am leaving myself behind.

18

WHEN THE DEBACLE HAPPENED with the switched test tubes, it was Silke's technician who had switched them. Silke felt terrible. She felt that it was all her fault. Screwing up her courage, she came to my father's office one afternoon and told him how terrible she felt and how she could not rid herself of the feeling that it was all her fault. My father consoled her. 'It's not your fault at all.' They felt terrible together and they had a drink together there in his office, in the late hours of the afternoon, consoling each other.

Dieter, Silke's husband, told my mother that their relationship had begun this way.

Perhaps Silke had fallen in love with my father long before, when he was still his old self, charismatic and charming; when he was the still young head of the laboratory and she the much younger associate, daunted by his intelligence, slowly gaining confidence in herself, flustered when he noticed her.

They drank together. They hid in his office. They imagined themselves as two children lost in the woods, holding hands.

*

For months my father was bursting with his news, with the desire to boast about his affair. It was on the tip of his tongue. He was filled with a sense of the importance of his secret; it was thrilling, awful, it possessed tremendous explosive potential. What would happen when it all came out? He was increasingly driven to drop tantalizing hints while still imagining that no one could possibly guess. Mysterious leftovers appeared in the refrigerator — half-eaten jars of Russian caviar, smoked eel, and similar delicacies, remnants of romantic picnics. When he was drunk my father boasted about his affair openly to my mother. Then, when he was sober again, he would deny everything, forgetting that he had already spilled the beans.

*

My mother found a slip of paper in a medical dictionary that told her that my father's hepatitis had not been hepatitis at all. Dr Uhland had colluded with him in concealing the true diagnosis from her.

*

There are two stories my mother told me later, that for many years I have been unwilling to let enter my imagination.

One is that during this time when my father was, as she put it, 'losing control', he used to sometimes go to the train station and share a bottle with one of the drunks there. I can picture the scene all too well, night-time, the lighting as on an intimate stage. My father childishly thrilled, the way he used to be when, as a Professor, he got a special pass to the town casino, otherwise open only to the Swiss who came from across the border. He is crossing a forbidden line. I wouldn't put it past him to affect as part of his disguise some special accent, his own terrible approximation of 'low' dialect, the way he used to talk to people in the market. He is flooded with warm feeling: the outcasts have accepted him as one of their own, clasped him in a fraternal embrace.

The great Professor has sunk so low — what will become of him?

The other story is that, at the same time as he was secretly meeting Silke, my father was also making advances to cleaning ladies in the laboratory building; writing billets-doux to an office girl. The grotesqueness of this pains me; I transfer it to the cleaning ladies, imagining for each of them some flaw — a rotted tooth, dark roots showing under bleached hair, pockmarked skin — which allows my father to maintain an ironic distance, conquering but never conquered. *The rake, he's just irresistible to women.* Silke, apparently, was jealous.

✳

I have a notion that, for a while at least, drinking must have given my father a sense of new-found freedom. Letting himself go, surrendering himself to free-fall, knowing with certainty that he was destroying himself and giving up everything he had wanted and worked for, he suddenly discovered himself marvellously light and without fear. It was a true adventure. He felt the happiness of embarkation, as if he were setting out by himself with a light knapsack to discover a new, dark and dangerous continent.

Perhaps in a strange way he felt it as a kind of beginning.

19

COMING HOME for Christmas in my second year at college, I experience a small nightmare at the airport in Zurich. I'm standing by the luggage conveyor belt waiting for my suitcase and trying to spot either of my parents among the crowd behind the glass partition. Suddenly, up against the glass, I see my father's black Russian fur hat — but underneath there is this horrible mask, large and white, with heavy-lidded eyes and an insanely widened mouth. It is my father, monstrously distorted! Moments later I see my father, a different man without a hat, at the back of the crowd.

*

My mother has changed. Her mouth has become set, its corners are pulled slightly downward by the lines meeting it from the sides of her nose. Gone are the diaphanous sunny curls framing an angelic face: her hair, darker and straighter than before, is pulled back and held by a clasp at her neck in a fashion that I find unattractive. Sitting in her chair in the living room, she ensconces herself behind *Newsweek*, books of history; she is accumulating hard facts, shoring up a bank of knowledge about the world to surround her like a fort. It's not that she hasn't tried to help my father; she's done everything she could. She's talked to him, pleaded with him; she wanted them to make a new beginning. While I was at college, they took a trip together that was supposed to mark this new beginning. He was sober the whole time, she could see how difficult it was for him and she did everything to distract him, to keep his mind filled with pleasant thoughts and sights. And then they came back and within a few days it had started all over again.

There is a change in her manner toward my father that is disturbing to me. She is acting compliant and almost meek; letting him get away with all kinds of things that would have made her angry before: not coming home for lunch, not coming home for dinner until eight o'clock, leaving food on his plate, etc. She seems completely indifferent, almost absent-minded, which I'm sure infuriates him. I resort to the same strategy: plunge my face into a camomile steam bath while he is trying to tell me about his students, interrupt him to ask my mother a question about something completely different.

I pretend to be so preoccupied that I scarcely notice my father's presence, when in fact the opposite is true. Especially when he is drunk, I feel that my nerves are drawn to him as by suction, fastened to him so that he can move me like a marionette. It's not a simple question of going along with his whims or not, of ignoring him when he sits at the head of the dinner table, eating his food in unbelievably slow motion and making remarks designed to disrupt our conversation. Even in having to resist him I feel I am being controlled by him.

There are small moments of liberation when my brother says something subtly ridiculing my father, who is too dulled and self-absorbed to notice the keen irony concealed in a seemingly innocuous remark; then my mother looks at my brother with laughing, rewarding eyes. I too try to enter this game.

How have the two of them survived this, day in day out? My brother seems the most immune to my father, the most aloof. He closes his door all the time, whereas I keep mine open, out of a compulsion to know and hear everything that goes on. Once, going into my brother's room, I see one of his school books open; in the margin he has written the words, *Out of it and moving on.*

Although my brother is sixteen, my mother has started again the practice of reading to him before he goes to bed, as she used to do when we were small children. They close the door and she sits on the edge of his bed in the lamplight (he has a new teddy bear, too) and they can forget everything for a while as they immerse themselves in *Watership Down.*

*

I pretend to be unshakeable. Nothing fazes me. In part this act is for my mother's benefit: 'Look, if I can do it, so can you.' My mother tells me that she is planning another trip to America in the spring, for two months, perhaps she will visit me at college. I say, somewhat sternly, that while she certainly deserves it, she should make it dependent on my father's progress, since it would be asking rather much of my sixteen-year-old brother to babysit an alcoholic father for so long. Even as a say it I wonder what exactly I mean by 'progress'.

She comes out of the kitchen and stands before me. 'You know,' she says, 'if he becomes an alcoholic, I am going to leave him when Martin is out of school. I have to stick with him for Martin's sake at least that long, but I don't want to be married to an alcoholic for the rest of my life.'

'You're right,' I say.

*

My father is distraught, hiding his face in his hands at dinner, pacing back and forth muttering, 'Oh *God* . . .' We pay no attention to him. It is as if he did not exist.

In the morning, an outburst of aggression toward my mother: 'She likes to have a *warm, friendly* breakfast, a fried *egg* that *stares* her in the *face.*' All my life we have been eating eggs for breakfast. It appears that my father would have preferred something else.

My mother says that the alcohol has 'eaten big holes into his brain'. It is true that he says intelligent things with increasing rarity. We must unconsciously feel sorry for him, because we hold back at the dinner table, when we could easily run circles around him. When we do win an easy victory, we are quick to gloss it over.

'You both,' he says to my mother and me, 'you both *criticize* me. And then I kick. I just start kicking!' He has what is meant to be a dangerous glint in his eye.

*

In the strained, insistent whisper that is reserved for big revelations, my father tells me: 'I *use* people . . .' He has also told me recently that, with regard to me, he is merely playing the role of a loving father, while observing himself as if from a distance.

He is casting himself now as a wicked betrayer of others' good faith, as an actor with the power to beguile others and make them do what he wants. Thus he attempts to create for himself a sort of isolation in evilness, which is better than destitution or helplessness.

With an air of someone begging for love, he tells me that he knows he bores my mother, he can feel her boredom even when she smiles politely. 'I can give only what I have,' he says, 'and if it *bores* people . . .' He is so shameless that he wants sympathy for his very inability to elicit affection. In the midst of our New Year's celebration (such as it is) he throws a full-blown tantrum, reproaching us with curses for our coldness, like a beggar who expects to be given money in return for clawing and scratching the passers-by.

*

Once again I am in bed, my door is slightly open, I've fallen asleep briefly and woken up to the sound of my parents' voices. I strain to listen. I overhear little bits. My mother: 'But you've wanted to have an affair for a long time.' My father: 'Yes, I *wanted* . . .' My mother: 'And I resent that.' There are a few exchanges that I can't make out and then I hear fragments of what my father is saying: 'Well, was it just the minister who was present? . . . The cutting of the wedding cake? . . . That's what I mean . . .'

My mother goes into their bedroom and I see her face as she passes my door. She's not crying, but her eyes are hard and angry and hurt as I've never seen them before. Usually she goes to bed before my father does, but tonight he has followed her into the bedroom, which means that he wants to continue talking. He is talking only to torture her. She has told me that when I am at college, she often comes to my bed in order to be able to sleep. But now I am here and she is trapped in there with him. I lie in my bed and have to listen. I can't simply roll over and go to sleep, even though now I can't make out any words: I have to continue to listen. Again his voice: why do I never hear hers? It's my duty to listen, to pay attention; it's wrong that I forget about it all as soon as I leave. My father's voice has an aggressive insistency, and I picture my mother lying there with the covers drawn up to her chin, her eyes closed, pretending that she is not paying any attention to him. He is standing in his underpants and pyjama top. How can she bear it? He comes out of the bedroom with an exclamation and his drunk, malevolent laugh; then he remembers something and goes back in, shutting the door behind him, to tell her.

*

It's my father's birthday. I am to leave again for college the next day. It's as though nothing had ever been amiss, as if it had all been a bad dream. Scenes like him and my mother standing in a silent, tight embrace; my mother chasing him playfully out of the kitchen when he tries to nibble from the cooking pots; both of them together trying to fix the head of my desk lamp; my father crying with laughter and surprise as our next-door neighbours lift up the chair on which he is sitting for a '*Hoch! hoch! hoch!*' What is going on? Is it a pretence of harmony trying to become genuine? The up following the down in a cyclic alternation? I no longer understand anything.

20

WHEN WE CROSSED the Atlantic on the *Europa*, I was too young to appreciate the full meaning of 'first class', but I remember now that the words did have a significance for me. And this was that I was allowed, once or twice, to wear a certain exciting, unbelievably beautiful dress that had appeared from who knows where in my wardrobe. Someone, certainly not my practical mother, had given me this dress; it must have been a hand-me-down. The colours in it were the colours of canned fruit cocktail, delicate peach orange, pears' yellow-white, the barely-green of grapes. It was made of some light, semi-transparent material, with a white slip underneath, and it was all narrow pleats from the stiff white collar down, so that it fluttered and swirled and lifted with the slightest movement. I was seven, I wore white lacy tights under this dress and – it was too perfect – shoes that were just the colour of fruit cocktail cherries.

I felt dazzling as I walked down the ship gangway. I was feverish with self-consciousness because I knew that all eyes must be drawn to me in admiration.

*

I am visiting my mother, looking at pictures in an album of hers that I haven't seen before. These photos have no colours, they're black-and-white: group shots taken on the *Europa* by the ship's photographer. They show my parents, along with a couple of other people who must have been their table companions. The women are wearing long gowns, the men suits or even tuxedos. But what a disappointment! How dreary, how pathetic it all looks, compared to the mythical glamour of that ship voyage. The sixties furniture, the tacky decor, deplorable hair styles (except my mother) . . . And to think that while I was lying in bed straining to hear the sounds that meant my parents' escape, while I was visualizing the awkwardness of boarding the little boat, the ropes let down, hands held out in dark of night, they were merely sitting like this around little tables with their cocktail glasses placed on little napkins, pudgy waiters in bow-ties proffering trays of caviar toast.

But what has really grabbed my attention in these photos – I'm merely stalling – is the man who is always sitting on my mother's *other* side. My father is on one side, and it's Irving, Irving whom I've come to know, much younger but already balding, unmistakable, who is on the other. In one shot all eyes are turned toward him, my father is even leaning forward to hear his anecdote. Probably Irving is not speaking loudly enough because it is for my mother's benefit that he is telling it, his head turned lightly in her direction. No, I'm not imagining things, even that blond man has eyes only for my mother in two of the three pictures; she was obviously the prize of the party, that's why his sari-wrapped Indian wife looks so disgruntled.

It's so strange to see these pictures now. Irving, the European-American, the *raconteur*. My father remembers him well, what a pain he was. It was always, 'May I join you? Do you mind?' Leaving his Midwestern Mary-Ellen behind, he cruised the Atlantic, attaching himself to my parents. According to my father they never had a moment alone together but he would invariably show up, following them around the ship.

Why did my mother keep in touch with him all those years?

There is more. Stuck inside the album, not attached, is a yellowed newspaper clipping. It shows a man in uniform, with a face like a wood carving, behind a podium. There are flags and flowers in the background; medals on the chest of his uniform. The caption is in a language I can't even identify: *Jopa välikysymys tentiin eduskunnassa, silloin kun Urheilujoukkoja perustettiin, kertoi evl Kalevi Römpötti juhlaesitelmässään.*

'Who's this?' I ask my mother, waving the clipping vaguely at her. 'Oh,' she says with studied casualness, 'that was an old boyfriend of mine in graduate school. He was from Finland, he was a track star. For years he used to send me Christmas cards, sometimes with little pressed flowers in them.' She says it in a lightly mocking tone, seemingly scoffing at his sentimentality. But at the bottom of the clipping she has pencilled the words, *Very last one*.

Römpötti was his name. It sounds like rum-pot. I conclude that Finnish is a grotesque language; but to me it's all grotesque: my mother and a track star, pressed flowers. Again and again I stare in disbelief at this clipping. It reminds me of something pickled – a thousand-year egg.

I know the loss of love is common, an everyday thing. Still, something compels me to pick up the shards; I clean them off carefully with a soft brush, arrange them in order. I try to understand how it happened.

*

I remember the day I became convinced that my mother had a secret, male friend. That morning, there had been three letters for her in the mail, one from my grandmother and two from a place in America, in the same handwriting, with no return address. My mother had stopped back from the laboratory before going to the grocery store and she had taken the two letters with her, leaving the one from her mother. They were in her purse now. She had had so many letters in the past weeks in that same handwriting.

I thought, 'She is still playing the victim, but she has already begun, quietly, to look out for herself.' I wanted to tell her that I knew about it in a way that would frighten her. I hated her stupidly feigned innocence. But instead I would have to pretend that I knew nothing, and when, much later, she would begin to break the news to me gently, I would have to pretend to be surprised and happy for her.

Living amidst all this deceit, I decided to become the best deceiver of all. I needed the utmost craftiness and cleverness to survive. From now on, I would be suspicious of everything. I would trust no one. I would watch and listen and hoard my knowledge, which gave me a lonely power.

*

That same day, my father came while my brother and I were having lunch; my mother had not yet returned from the grocery store. My father had recently moved out of our apartment, first into a hotel, now into Silke's house.

'I came to unpack my suitcase and get some different clothes.'

I said that my mother would be coming back soon.

'If she can't stand my presence, she will just have to go away. — I'm going to put on a record.'

My brother went into his room. My father lit a cigarette. 'You know, she came into my office this morning, and she was shaking like a leaf.'

'Please don't stay long,' I said. 'I don't want to see her shaking like a leaf.'

'She couldn't bear the sight of me.' He then started saying how he had nowhere to go. 'NOWHERE TO GO!'

I made some moralizing statement about taking responsibility for one's own deeds, and told him not to wallow in self-pity. 'I too have nowhere to go,' I said righteously, 'in the sense that home is the last place on earth I want to be right now.'

'But I *like* it here,' he said. 'I haven't heard music for weeks!' He had put on the *Appassionata*. 'I am trying not to wallow in self-pity,' and his eyes become moist with self-pity, 'I am just trying to survive. Just to survive.' Then, pleading: 'I didn't want things to turn out this way. Do you believe me?'

While he went into the shower, I took the cellar key and hid it.

Afterwards he came to my room to say, 'Maybe she won't come in as long as she sees my car outside.' His voice was full of fear. I felt sorry for him: quaking at the thought of what he had done. To reassure him, I told him she had probably gone on to do some errands.

'I'm going to get ready and leave now,' he said.

But my mother came while he was still there. They started fighting immediately, without any preliminary. It wasn't like their fighting used to be, each of them full of rage and passion. It was something automatic and habitual now. My father trying all the same devices over and over – entreaties, threats – in a desperate hope against hope that they could still be effective; my mother stony, retreating behind a wall of invariable, impermeable coldness.

My father had told me a few days ago that each morning now his first thought was: 'Dear God, let it not be true.' I imagined him saying this on waking up next to Silke.

*

At the end of my mother's photo album, where our family life ended, she began putting in miscellaneous photos that she had received from other people: Christmas cards, photos of other families, other couples and their children.

21

It is a sunny, beautiful spring day. I am riding the bicycle that Silke has lent me through a quiet residential street not far from the house in which we used to live. All the gardens are in fullest bloom, as if for my benefit, to welcome me. I feel a quiet ecstasy of recognition; at the same time I am tense, anticipating that the recognition will be returned, that I will meet someone who will remember me. But I meet no one. I'm glad, this is the way I want it to be. I am incognito, or even invisible.

Once, walking in this same neighbourhood, I saw a boy whose face, even though I had forgotten him for well over a decade, seemed like the face of a long-lost friend. He was grown now too, of course, but he still looked the same. He recognized me as well. *Hallo!* we greeted each other enthusiastically. The next instant I remembered that he was retarded. I didn't know his name and I had never talked to him before.

The people I encounter when I come back are always those who were most peripheral to my life, whom I never gave a second thought, much less expected ever to see again. A sallow teller at the bank has the greatest permanence; I see him again and again, at intervals of years. I know he recognizes me too, but neither of us lets it show. It's like those dreams in which someone I barely know suddenly plays an important role, giving me advice or rescuing me from danger. I feel as though these people were the skeleton, the bleached bare bones that were there all along underneath the fleshed-out shape of my experience.

Following my old route to school, I ride through a little stretch of woods. My muscles seem still to know the way, accelerating and slowing down in all the right places, leaning into the curves at just the right angle. These woods, cool, dark, and moist, smelling richly of mushrooms, were our playground when we were little. Frau Blume used to take my brother and me here and we built houses for trolls out of stones and bark. Somewhere, though I would not be able to find it any more, there is a narrow path we used to call the bicycle wash, because of the wet branches that brushed you on either side; in another place we used to test our daring, riding down an incline so steep that it gave us enough speed to ride up another, equally steep incline on the other side.

Downtown, I make a point of doing everything a little differently from my old habits. I go to the other bookstore; to the small stationer's shop instead of the large one where things are cheaper. I relish the polite, ritual interaction with store owners: *Guten Tag, Vielen Dank, Auf Wiedersehen*. I am a spy who has mastered the local accent perfectly.

In my interactions with my father, I am cocooned in layers of resistance, anaesthetized, swathed in shock-absorbant cotton wool. I still can't really face him. The person with the breezy manner who talks and looks at him is not me but some kind of effigy of myself.

I am grateful for Silke's presence. She seems to have a good influence. We are all polite, they spoil me like an honoured guest; and everything is fine.

*

My father tells me that his latest research excites him. After all these years, some recent experiments seem to point to something important. 'It's real,' he says. 'It's not my imagination.' Is he trying to persuade me or himself? 'There's a group in Basel who are on the same track. I have to hurry.'

I know what he wants. He hopes to make a final splash, one last big discovery that will dazzle the scientific community. To be able to say, 'See, and you had already written me off, you came here with your funeral speeches, but I've surprised you all!'

He is investigating a phenomenon called *apoptosis*. 'You should know what that means, with your Greek,' he says, ' "leaves falling off of trees", or something like that.' Cells simply die, spontaneously, without any external cause. It's a programmed death; no one knows yet why or by what mechanism it occurs. In the microscope you can clearly distinguish cells that are well from cells that are dying. Healthy cells have a smooth, round outline, while the walls of dying cells fold in and out so that they look like little flowers. The design on Silke's dress is driving him crazy, he adds, laughing. The flowers on it remind him constantly of his research.

I am struck by this connection of death and flowering: 'flowering' not in the sense of a natural blossoming, but in the sense of becoming — suddenly, at the last moment — complicated, intricate and involuted.

My father has brought photos from the lab, made with a fluorescence microscope. 'Are you *sure* you want to see them?' He is being coy: he is eager to show them to me. In fact, they are beautiful. Three different dyes were used; some are bright turquoise, others fiery red, others a rich golden ochre. 'Now,' he says, spreading them out on the coffee table, shuffling them, lovingly rearranging them. 'In this one you see cells that are healthy, nothing wrong with them. Nice, round, happy cells. And here – isn't this dye just incredible? that we can actually photograph something like this? – here, you can see something is happening . . .'

I listen anxiously, interrupting him often with questions, looking for a logical flaw. In the back of my mind I am convinced he is deluding himself, setting himself up for a fall. He seems too enamoured of the beauty of the pictures. 'My goodness but you're persistent!' he exclaims with a laugh, when I've been nagging him with my questions. 'She doesn't let up. She's really tough.'

This to Silke, who sits on the sofa watching us.

'You have some other pictures,' Silke says to my father with her sphinx-like smile. 'Don't you want to show them to Irene, too?'

'Nooo, do you really think I should?'

'You've shown them to everyone else.'

While he goes upstairs to look for them, Silke tells me that they are pictures taken just after he was stung by a wasp a few months ago. 'Actually, he loves to show them to people.'

Although I think I am prepared for the worst I am not prepared for what I see. My father is sitting at his desk in these shots, turning back toward the camera. His entire head is blown up like a balloon. The wrinkles under his eyes are inflated into full, protruding pouches; the cheeks are enormous. He is unrecognizable. 'Someone said he looks like Chairman Mao,' Silke says.

Even his lips, which in some photos he has drawn out into a ghastly grin, are puffed out.

He was riding his bicycle one evening when suddenly he felt the wasp in his collar, trapped; a second later, trying to shoo it out with his hand, he felt its sting. He stopped and got off his bicycle. A university acquaintance happened to come by and my father asked him to wait with him for a few minutes.

'Of course, the thing one fears will happen in such cases is that the swelling will close off the trachea.' My father accompanies this statement, delivered in a coolly scientific tone, with a gesture to his throat. 'But after three minutes I knew that the allergic reaction would have passed its peak and I was going to be OK. So I got back on my bike and rode home. This is what I looked like three hours later.'

The photographs couldn't be more terrifying or ugly if they showed a bloated corpse. I have no doubt my father intends to use them in his last immunology lectures, or perhaps has already done so. He enjoys the shock they produce: gleefully, like a child wearing a scary mask. He means to show that, no matter how outwardly repulsive and unrecognizable he may become, his real self sits above it all, aloof and untouched, regarding the transformation clinically.

And yet as I stare at the pictures, transfixed, I can't help feeling that they reveal something he shouldn't have wanted to reveal. That leering, swollen visage, flouting death, is not a mask.

*

The three of us, Silke, my father, and I, watch a show on TV that happens to come on after the news. It's about animals in Africa. A terrible drought has brought all sorts of different species together at a watering hole, and the photographer has only to sit and wait to capture them all. The grass-eating animals, especially the smaller, weaker ones, become easy prey for the carnivorous beasts, who thus find not only water but a ready feast at the watering hole. A narrator is explaining this situation placidly while the film shows birds, gazelles, giraffes, zebras, elephants, hyenas, leopards, and lions, all brought together by thirst. One scene shows a recently born baby elephant that doesn't know what to do with its trunk. It is visibly puzzled and irritated by the long appendage in front of its face; it seems to want to flick it off, then twirls it round and round like a propeller. We can't help laughing at it. The charming nature of this scene, together with the sanguine tone of the narrator, who seems scarcely able to contain his joy over such photographic serendipity, makes me feel certain that pretty soon the rain will begin to fall and the drought will be ended and the animals will go their separate ways. It all seems set up for a happy ending. But instead, the film begins to show large groups of animals dying. Soon the dried-up watering hole is surrounded by corpses. The baby elephant lies by its mother's side, weakly lifting its trunk in a last sign of life.

The lions are among the last to survive in force, because they are able to glean moisture from the carcasses of the other animals for a while. But even this does not last long. The final sequence shows a pack of about six lions stalking a tough old buffalo. The buffalo is much bigger and stronger than the lions, and so, rather than attacking it immediately, they surround it and slowly, gradually unnerve it. Had it remained standing still in one spot, the lions might never have been able to get the better of it; but it loses its nerve and begins to run. This is its fatal mistake. The biggest of the male lions leaps from behind, fastening its teeth with all its might in the buffalo's hindquarters. It clings to the buffalo like this, teeth sunk into flesh, for almost an hour while the buffalo heaves and rocks, rears and bucks and shakes itself furiously from side to side, expending little by little its tremendous store of energy. When at last it begins to flag, another lion, the second largest male in the pack, attacks, biting into the buffalo's neck.

Now the end comes quickly. When the buffalo is dead, the remaining lions approach the carcass to eat, in order of rank. The first and choicest shreds are brought to the old male, who has held on to the buffalo's flank for so long that he is too exhausted to tear them off for himself.

'By the way,' my father says, apropos of nothing. 'I had a thorough physical check-up recently and the doctor told me that I'm in very good health.' He says this with a strange, punishing emphasis: reproaching me for not having enquired. It sounds as if he meant to say: 'In case you're hoping for me to drop dead, don't expect it to happen any time soon!'

*

Over the years my feelings about Silke have changed; I have grown to like her. But there is still a core of something incomprehensible to me. I do not understand her relationship with my father. What is their life, what keeps them going on?

One afternoon my father comes back from the lab in a sober and irritable mood. He begins reproaching Silke, saying that she ought to take more responsibility for the care of a certain strain of mice. She retorts that it is someone else's job; they argue. Although I have no idea what it's all about, I inwardly take Silke's side at once. My father is technically her boss, but the thought that he should try to tell her, or anyone, what to do, seems to me an outrage. Doesn't he realize that he's on borrowed time, that Silke's tolerance, the world's tolerance of him could run out at any moment? I am completely disgusted;

I go downstairs and lie on my bed, glad that I am leaving soon. Shortly afterwards, my father comes and sits on the edge of my bed and gently apologizes for his behaviour. 'I had a tough day.' For some reason this apology makes me even angrier. I'm not the one to whom he should apologize. He is treating me as if I were sensitive and had been hurt, when really I am hard and contemptuous. 'I don't care about that,' I say, sitting up. 'I was lying down because my throat hurt. I should probably gargle with salt.' My father then tells me that when he feels a cold coming on, he doesn't merely gargle with salt water, he *inhales* it, draws it up his nostrils.

The thought of this grotesque, fanatical remedy is so comical that it appeases me. I am eager to try it at once. It reminds me of other old-fashioned German remedies: of our neighbour who, seeing my brother's pallor as a little boy, recalled that she had been made to drink her own urine 'to bring a little red to her cheeks'; or the cruel cartoon stories of Wilhelm Busch, the woman who scorched her husband with a flat-iron after he had caught cold.

*

My father has been complaining of stomach trouble and also of low blood pressure. He must be taking blood pressure pills, for Silke will say, 'Why don't you take a pill?'

'I've already taken two today,' he'll respond. 'It says on the prescription you're only supposed to take two a day.'

Silke fusses and soothes. 'Shall I make you some tea?' she asks.

'But then I'll be up again all night.' She gets up and rummages in the kitchen for some peppermint tea, without caffeine. There is none, but a little later, as my father continues to look miserable, she says, 'I think I'll make you a little tea after all. If I make it very weak, it won't keep you up.'

'Ah, this feels good,' my father says when she has brought out his cup, taking careful sips of the hot liquid. 'Oh, this is really making me feel a lot better. Oh, yes, I'm starting to feel much better now. Thank you so much.'

Soon he feels so much better that he can pour himself a glass of wine, eat a chocolate biscuit, and pronounce his enjoyment of the evening.

I watch these exchanges and I don't know what to think.

*

My father saying to Silke, at the dinner table, in some trivial context: 'You can't get rid of me *that* easily.'

*

One afternoon, without warning, Silke has begun to talk to me about my father. Under the pretext of taking me shopping, she has created an opportunity to be alone with me. We're sitting in a coffee shop and suddenly she is saying, 'I've sometimes thought that I can't bear it anymore . . . to go on living with him . . . He can keep it under control for periods of time, it's true, he'll drink moderately for a while and then he'll say, "See? It's not a problem." But then again he'll feel a need to drink himself to oblivion . . . Especially when he goes to Collina by himself, he uses this as an opportunity . . . The last time he came back from Collina his delirium tremens was so bad that the entire bed was shaking. An acquaintance of ours once visited him down there. He told me, "A little more and he would have been dead." Last year it reached a point where I felt I really needed to talk to someone. I thought, if I don't talk to someone now, I'll go crazy. But I couldn't think of anyone to talk to. I thought of Erika and Gerhard, but I couldn't. And then it sort of passed. I've wanted to talk to you or Martin about it for a long time . . .

'It's got so that when I go to pick him up at the train when he comes back from Collina I dread the moment of seeing him step off. And then he'll say something like, "Why, aren't you glad to see me at all?" At times like this,' Silke tells me, 'I feel that I am a small helpless rabbit, and he is a big evil snake wanting to destroy me.'

The thought of Silke's loneliness shakes me to the core. It's on the tip of my tongue to say, 'Leave him, get away!' But I don't, I say other things instead. In the end she tells me she feels better now that we've spoken about it. 'I'm going to tell him that we've talked, if you don't mind, because I think it's only fair that he know.'

*

Near the end of my visit, my father asks me to help him with the translation of a business letter to Italy. I offer to type it while I'm at it, and he says I can use the typewriter in his room. I've asked him earlier if I could see his room, but he looked uneasy and said, 'No, not yet, it's too messy. I'll clean it up and then you can see it.'

Now, stepping inside, I instantly feel sorry that he has had to show it to me. The room used to be his study but I see that it has become 'his room' in another sense: half of it is taken up by his bed. Tiny, pressed down by a low sloping ceiling under the roof, the room was crowded before; but now, with the desk and the bicycle, one can't move. At the foot of the bed there is just enough space for two shelves containing his collection of microscopes. They jostle each other, all shapes and sizes, dozens of darkly shining brass and silver instruments.

'I can look at my microscopes when I lie in bed,' my father says in a joking way, gesturing toward the shelf.

'That's nice,' I manage to reply, with equally feigned lightness. I pretend not to care about anything around me; to be concerned only with my job of typing the letter.

My father's room is like a little child's room, a *Kinderzimmer*, with all the treasures crowded around the bed.

22

ONCE, when I was leaving for college, my father grabbed hold of me in the front doorway and kissed me hard on the mouth. It was a wilful, peremptory gesture, a fierce statement, intended to leave an impression not so easily wiped away.

*

At a train station in Italy, some time ago, I watched a father and a daughter saying goodbye to each other. I was sitting on the train; they were on the platform just outside my window. The daughter looked about my age, early thirties. The father had visited her, for the day or perhaps for the weekend, and now she was seeing him off.

They had sat down on a bench together and were talking. I couldn't hear what they were saying, I could only see them, their faces, their gestures. It was the daughter who was doing most of the talking, with a bright, animated expression, as if now, at the train station, during their last five or ten minutes together, she could still think of so many things to tell her father, or to ask him. He responded with a sort of weary smile, looking at her – how? His mouth smiled, but the rest of his face did not.

Without intending to, I was watching them closely. I saw that the daughter was acting, there was a false girlishness in her manner. Everything about her was false, desperately simulated, which gave her a strange, fluttering instability. It was all there for me to see: the manic animation, the affectionate embrace just before he got on the train, the little wave, the fraudulent smile, the way she came running back as if she had remembered one last thing. The second little wave, the smile, the springiness in her step.

I didn't have to see the daughter's expression as she walked down the platform away from me. When the father took a seat in my compartment, I saw in his thick-skinned drinker's face the hard look of someone who does not deceive himself.

*

My father stands on the platform and I wave to him energetically as my train pulls slowly away. He waves back, but mechanically, as if his heart weren't in it. His mind has already retreated from me, retracted like a snail into that dark place of its own. He has already forgotten me. He grows smaller with distance but I can still see his face clearly and it is blank, washed clean. I am still smiling but he no longer sees me.

When he is out of sight I sit back and open the envelope he pressed at the last moment into my hand. I count the money that is inside.

Part Two

23

New Haven, February 1996

I try to imagine Collina as it is now, at this very moment, or rather as it was six hours ago, when it was early morning there as it is here now. Early morning, thousands of miles away on the other side of the Atlantic. The sky streaked with red, the valley basin still filled with white cloud while Collina is perched above, in piercingly clear air, like a house on the shore of a sea of white.

It's still winter, so it is cold and the hills are brown. I see the brownish-red shutters tightly closed over all the windows and doors, the fieldstone walls, with bits of brick patched in here and there, dark and textured from the moisture of the night. I pass through these walls into the emptiness of the kitchen. It is all dark, cold, immobilized in a deep, months-old silence. Perhaps the espresso pot was left in the dish drainer by the sink, taken apart into its various components, all bone-dry by now and ice-cold. But the kitchen floor is moist as it is even in the heat of summer; the red clay tiles are saturated with moisture that soaks up into them from the ground below.

I can see everything now. I can smell the house, I can feel it. There are the terrace chairs folded up and leaning against the wall; the refrigerator left open, the table and all the kitchen utensils covered with plastic according to the established rituals of departure, to protect them from mouse and bat droppings. Because really the house isn't as empty as all that, as I was imagining it just now. It is full of life, full of creatures that make no sound – bats that swoop down through the chimney and sleep in the bedrooms upstairs, hanging like pears from the rafters; mice that, gnawing through plastic, build their nests everywhere; scorpions and centipedes and spiders. The house belongs to them.

When our household was dismantled, Collina became a receptacle for leftovers from our life. There were some pieces of furniture that neither of my parents wanted. My brother and my father together transported them across the Alps in a rented truck, taking turns driving. According to Martin, my father periodically refreshed himself along the way with red wine that he had decanted into a large pickle jar. He acted bewildered and offended when my brother protested. Apparently he had believed that the vessel could disguise its contents.

I find out now that in the first years after my mother returned to America, my father went to Collina every month, compulsively, even in the winter, in the cold. He put up pictures of the house in his office, as if clinging to the thought of it. Over the years he has continued to make improvements to it: a stone pavement for the terrace, a new floor in the front room, larger containers to collect the water that comes as a tiny trickle from a faraway spring. It's as if the house somehow embodied the intact version of our family. As if by continuing to go there, by paying the electricity bills year round, the property taxes, the nominal sum required to keep the telephone wire alive, my father were symbolically pronouncing his loyalty to the very thing that he destroyed.

And my mother, even now, in America, has never been able completely to break the habit of collecting things for Collina. Although she has no way of carrying them to Italy, her cellar is filling up with plates, coffee pots, knife stands.

Every summer my father asks me to spend time in Collina with him. I always refuse.

*

I've begun writing about my father, about us, in order to keep alive something that started in me when I saw his picture in that newspaper clipping. It's not much more for now than a hope of movement, a possibility of development. I am feeling my way into the story as into a lightless cave or underground tunnel, relying only on a sense of touch to read the contours of the terrain that surrounds me.

I am still using the old desk that my father helped me to restore, decades ago; I am writing on it now, in the early morning, drinking my tea as always. I remember the care with which we prepared the surface for the leather inset, sanding the wood until it felt like silk and bevelling the edges so that the leather would fit snugly. He stroked it when it was smooth and ready, the way he would stroke any beautifully crafted object.

A few minutes ago, taking tea leaves out of the tin with my fingers, I suddenly realized I was repeating exactly my father's gesture, the way he used to take a pinch of pipe tobacco out of his pouch.

The memories do not come willingly, I have to tease them out, to trick myself: I've worked hard in the past to forget things. Reading my old diaries gives me a peculiar sensation because often there is no memory attached to what I read, it's almost like reading the diaries of another person. In the spaces between entries there are sometimes memories of other incidents, but more often blanks, nothing.

I bring a notebook with me when I travel; I've been writing this in many different places, in different cities. I like to sit in cafés, watching other people as I write. There is a sort of dialogue between the scenes around me and those I am writing down. As I remember, or imagine, or invent a scene from the past, something completely different is unfolding before my eyes: Mr Li washing dishes with great dignity, wearing red rubber gloves; or Paolo solemnly, almost sadly pouring frothed milk into a cup of coffee; or a flirtation; or a young couple breaking up. I like to think that these things enter into the writing somehow; that they help to form it and are encoded there secretly as another layer of memory, a ghostly palimpsest, a bit like my aunt Erika's painted lines that continue invisibly on the back of the canvas.

* * *

The last time I saw my father in Collina was a few years after my parents' separation. It had been Erika's idea to visit him there. She and Gerhard had met up with me in Italy on their vacation and when she heard that he was staying there by himself, she was immediately aflame with her plan.

'We'll have dinner and spend the night, and then we'll leave the next day. Yes, why not, let's do it! There are enough beds for all of us, aren't there?'

Somewhere half-consciously I knew it was a mistake. But I said nothing, I merely called my father to announce our coming, and it was settled.

It was late afternoon when we arrived. As we drove up the last steep piece of road to the house, I saw my father standing at the top of the hill, waiting for us. I knew at that moment it was going to be even worse than I had feared. I could tell from his posture – the legs slightly bent at the knees so that he seemed to be leaning backward – that he was very drunk.

We got out of the car and he embraced me impetuously, awkwardly knocking our bodies together and blindly kissing my face, to make up for the constraint he felt in greeting his younger sister and Gerhard, who shook his hand formally.

'I just cut myself,' my father announced then, holding up his left index finger, which bulged with an enormous bandage of gauze and flesh-coloured tape.

'It was bleeding just incredibly. I could hardly get it to stop. I must have cut it deeply. I'm still not quite over the shock.'

So he was an invalid, wounded: I registered this with annoyed recognition, as if I should have foreseen he would do something like this; as if he'd done it on purpose. Stepping inside the house, I saw large brownish spots and splashes on the floor. They formed a line which appeared to lead up the stairs to the second floor. While my father summoned the others straight through the kitchen to the terrace at the back – 'The sun is just setting, you must come quickly!' – I followed this blood trail under the pretext of taking our suitcases upstairs.

The line veered from the right of the steps – where he had turned the corner, coming from the kitchen – to the left, and then back to the right. At the top landing it was momentarily lost as he had perhaps stood, confused, holding his right hand cupped under the bleeding finger. Where were the first-aid things kept? He had made a dash first into one bedroom and then another. The trail ended in the bathroom sink, in a gory mess of spattered red and cigarette ash.

The red in the sink was not more blood, as I first thought, but mercurochrome, which he had splashed on liberally, his hand shaking, his cigarette still in his mouth. Several cigarettes had been extinguished and the butts left on the shelf above the sink, along with the still open mercurochrome bottle. I stood staring at this scene for a moment, at once horrified and satisfied by my discovery. It occurred to me that it was not through oversight or his usual distraction that he had neglected to run water in the sink, but out of a wish to preserve what I was looking at now, not to wash away the memory of it quite yet.

And now I understood the ruthlessness of our announced visit: how the anticipation of it must have weighed on him, constricted him, sat in the pit of his stomach; how the mere thought of it must have destroyed his cherished privacy, the intimate freedom of his solitary drinking. How he must have feared and resented our intrusion. So that the cut finger – he had perhaps been fumbling with the kitchen knife, nervously awaiting our arrival – in a strange way provided a kind of diversion. Part of him was pleasurably excited by it; he enjoyed the dramatic effect of the blood spurting out. *I could bleed to death.* My father had stood here in front of the mirror for some time, judging by the number of cigarettes, absorbed in this drama in which he was both actor and audience, filled with awe and pity at the spectacle of his own suffering. Our arrival had been reduced to a secondary, ancillary event.

I hastily cleaned the sink and shelf and hurried downstairs to join the others. The sun had just set. 'You missed it,' said my father with exaggerated sorrowfulness. 'That's OK,' I replied coldly. 'There will be other sunsets. – Is there anything in the house we can cook?'

'But of course!' Reproachfully: what did I think? 'I went to the butcher's!' And he produced from the refrigerator a white paper packet which he proceeded to undo with the grandiosity of a magician pulling a rabbit from a hat. '*Bistecca fiorentina!*' Inside were four enormous slabs of meat, each one of which must have cost a fortune. He picked the packet up by the corners of the paper and let it fall again with a dull thud. It was a gesture of reckless generosity, as if to say: 'There: take it. It's nothing to me.'

What he actually said was, 'I don't know how to cook them, however.'

'I'll cook,' I said, my spirits lifting somewhat. I saw a refuge in competence, in scrounging for things to go with the steak, cooking, setting the table festively . . . We would get through the evening somehow. Somehow, if only he would go outside now and talk to Erika and Gerhard for half an hour, somehow, then, things would turn out all right. What I vaguely envisioned was imposing our own shape on the evening, a shape so positive and definite that it would absorb my father, assimilate him, render him innocuous.

But as I went about my preparations, I felt on one level a strange, almost gleeful suspense: like a child with a chemistry set, standing with shining eyes over a mixture that is certain to explode in her face.

*

And then we were sitting around the table with our plates before us and my father was asking: *Warum?* Again and again, like an incantation: '*Warum?* Why did I buy this house, I keep asking myself? *Warum?* What for?'

At first, when he had started in, ponderously, wistfully, his voice sodden, his questions had got lost in our cheerful dinner table chatter. By an unspoken consent we decided to ignore them. 'It'll pass,' we thought. 'He'll get over it.' We tried to include him, to draw him into our conversation. We addressed different questions to him to soothe him and help him out of his difficulty. But he must have felt this. He must have sensed our complicity and rebelled. He persisted: '*Warum?* What is it all for? What does it mean?'

Now an embarrassed silence had fallen and it was like a draw or a stalemate. I couldn't help feeling that he had us where he wanted. We sat looking at each other around the table, or maybe not daring to look at each other but looking instead at our plates, the glasses, or beyond the table into the dimly lit room. Even if my father was too drunk to have complete control over his movements (a moment ago he had nearly upset the wine bottle in putting it down, and he was spilling half of his food on the place mat), even if his left eye was bloated and brimming, oozing tears that he occasionally wiped at with the back of his hand – still there was a sort of cunning left in him, with which he fought against us all. I don't even remember what we had been talking about. Our whole conversation was at that moment erased, cancelled, swept aside.

The room in which we were sitting was one of the least restored in the house. The floor was covered with greyish industrial tiles; the walls had splotches on them and areas of chipped paint, with cornflower blue coming through from the bottom, speckling the white that covered it. The lighting came from a heavy wrought-iron lamp that had an upturned basket for a shade. I remember being amazed, throughout the evening, at the design it cast on the walls – an enormous, intricate spider's web of light reaching all the way from the ceiling to the floor.

'The solitude isn't good for me. It's too much — even I, who like to be by myself, can't stand so much solitude. Such complete silence all the time. It scares me. And yet I come here . . .'

To my right, out of the lamp's reach, was the fireplace, dark and cavernous. It was big enough for a family to cluster within it: there was even a little stone bench on one side. This was one of the things that had most delighted Martin and me when, as children, we had explored the house for the first time. We had taken turns sitting on the bench, imagining what it would be like to warm ourselves by the fire, with the smoke going up into the dark hole of the chimney above. The fireplace was all dusty now and filled with cobwebs. A strange old mouldy basket and a square clay tile on which I had painted a chessboard one summer had ended up in it, along with an iron kettle and some antique implements that my mother had collected. The chimney was used only by the bats. It was their entry and exit during the long months when the house stood empty.

'Don't you come here to relax, to restore your spirits?'

'Because it's so beautiful up here . . .'

It was Erika who went along with him first, trying to respond reasonably to his questions. She regarded her elder brother with simple-hearted admiration, and was lost and distressed at seeing him in this state. She wanted to cheer him up.

Gerhard would have seconded her: 'Perhaps you shouldn't come here alone.' And, with a friendly grin: 'I can imagine it could be kind of spooky staying here all alone.'

'Yes!' my father shouts. 'Spooky — God knows it is that!'

And at this point he tells about the time when the silence was so intense that all he could hear was the ticking of the kitchen clock. Soon he could think of nothing but its ticking; until he suddenly reached up and grabbed it down from the wall and removed the battery.

'And at night, you know, I always keep a weapon by the side of my bed, either a sickle, or the *zappa*. It's irrational, the fear I have after a couple of days when I am here by myself.'

His voice rumbles, he laughs as if he were crying, sniffs loudly and wipes the tears from his eyes with the back of his hand. He pours more wine for himself and offers it to the rest of us.

'*So why, why do I keep coming here, again and again?*'

'You come here because you want to,' I say coldly, my unsympathetic tone jarring with Erika's anxious solicitude, Gerhard's practical concern. I knew that my father's questions were not real questions, not meant to be answered. He didn't care about any of the answers that Erika and Gerhard, meaning well, were trying to provide.

He ignores me; he is on the subject of money now. 'I have to pay, and pay, and pay, just to keep the house from tumbling down. I just got the bill today for the repairs to the roof. It's bleeding me dry. And for what? Just so that I have something to leave to my children? I have nothing else to leave to them. But is it worth it?'

Underneath, incredibly, is the feeling that it is he who has been abandoned by us, his family. We have all gone off to America, leaving him with the burden of maintaining this bat-infested mausoleum of memories, this monument to old dreams of a simple and beautiful life. He has become its lonely caretaker.

'You only come here as *vacationers*, for little *visits*, a little *overnight*.' This last is spat out in my direction with wrathful vehemence, as exaggerated as the self-pity a moment before.

'Then why don't you sell it?'

Call his bluff. Not that it's his decision to make alone; it's my mother's too. But it's a lie that he is keeping Collina for us, a martyr to his children. He would cling to it for dear life. He would never give it up. It has become his precious hideaway, where he can drink freely, unencumbered, far from watching, accusing eyes.

I had said it mockingly, my voice icy with the contempt and revulsion I felt for him at that moment. But my aunt and uncle were now both eagerly taking up this proposition: to sell the house that was causing so much grief. 'Yes, why don't you sell it? *Um Gottes Willen,* I'm sure your children would understand!' Erika had tears in her eyes, with relief that so simple a solution had been found. 'Sell it, by all means! Sell it right away!' And Gerhard, in his thoughtful way, said, 'I don't see why not, under the circumstances . . .'

This is not how my father wanted things to go. A practical solution is not what he is looking for. He ignores it. He has to start from a new angle, select a point of attack that lies deeper and closer to home, where it can't be isolated in this clinical, commonsensical way.

His voice is deep and slow and wistful. 'And then, when I am here by myself I start to get depressed. I start thinking bad thoughts. In a few years it will be time for me to retire. In general I am looking forward to retirement – I've earned it, by God . . . But I can't help asking myself, what will I be good for any more? What meaning will my life have?'

The questions fall leadenly, one by one, into the silence.

'What is left for me to do? What do I live for?'

A kind of panic had gripped me from the moment we arrived. It gave me a strange sense of clairvoyance, as though I had insect eyes through which the confused reality of what was going on was broken into a million separate facets, each of glittering precision. It was clear to me that this moment was a battle. I felt, oddly, as though I had somehow brought it about deliberately, orchestrated the whole thing. I had known something like this would happen; I could have prevented it. But instead I had brought my aunt and uncle here on purpose, to help me fight against my father.

He seemed to me to be driven by a deep anger. There was something very powerful about him even now. He had contrived to turn his very weakness into a weapon. It was his own horribly drunken state with which he confronted us as an irrefutable argument, his own dissolution becoming a kind of dissolving agent, destroying any positive, practical, life-affirming conviction like a corrosive chemical. When he asked, *What am I good for any more?*, putting his own ruin before us like an open wound, paradoxically we were the desperate ones, not he. We were desperate and somehow comically pathetic as we put forth our little philosophies of positive thinking: *learn to enjoy life, take an interest, not personal achievement or greatness* . . . Our voices sounded lost, like the squeaking of mice. Our assertions had a tinny, artificial ring. The very eagerness with which we said these things undermined them.

*

I don't remember how it was that the evening finally ended. I don't think any of us slept that night. Terrible noises kept coming from my father's room, mutterings and a strange piteous moaning. Behind his closed door he had turned into something which the mind shrank from imagining. Was he awake or asleep? Hour after hour, in that house surrounded by all the most peaceful sounds of the countryside, the heart-rending noises continued from my father's bedroom.

24

THE SUMMER AFTER my parents separated, I remember I went to visit Frau Blume one afternoon in her apartment. She had baked a crumb cake in my honour; it was accompanied by the inevitable reminder of how in the past, when she used to bake crumb cakes at our house, 'I'd turn my back and when I looked again, half the sheet was gone — you'd eaten it before it had even cooled!' We sat surrounded by her knick-knacks and mementoes and I quickly realized that she had invited me with a purpose: to talk about my parents. I dug into my cake and she dug into her topic. 'This is the way I see it,' she said, after a brief pretence of asking my opinion. 'I don't think you should blame your father. He is a noble man. Your mother is a good person too, very thrifty and hard-working. I don't know anyone as hard-working as your mother. But maybe your father would rather have had a German wife, after all.'

For a few moments I was struck speechless by the sheer, baffling stupidity of her remark, and the disloyalty toward my mother, who had always treated her so well. I was hurt by the image that presented itself of our old beloved Frau Blume gossiping with her wrinkled and deeply tanned friends as they lounged by the lakeside, discussing my parents' scandal as if it were a story in *Bunte Illustrierte*, enjoying the special insider's knowledge that she had. I realized that she had invited me over to fish for extra titbits.

'I've heard that this other woman is very elegant, is that true? Some men just prefer an elegant woman, with expensive tastes, to a thrifty one. You have to understand that.'

*

My brother stayed in Germany the longest but eventually he came to live in New York. He is a painter. The two of us are much closer today than we ever were as children. 'You were out of there quicker than lightning,' Martin tells me now, looking back. 'You were gone.' He has this memory from the time after my father moved out, when it was just the two of them, he and my mother, living in our apartment. In the evenings my mother used to sit, as always, in her chair reading. For some reason now she'd turn off all the other lights in the apartment, possibly to save money, leaving only her reading lamp burning. Martin would go out with his friends at night; but this image of her sitting in her small pool of light, surrounded by darkness, came with him as a burden of guilt.

Facing the blank uncertainty of her future, my mother says that she thought to herself, 'No matter where I go or what happens to me, it can't be worse than this.' She lives in the Midwest now. She does research in a laboratory at the university where Irving teaches. She has returned to her old interest, the brain. Instead of fish she now studies the brains of rats.

I've dropped out of graduate school in order to do what I always secretly wanted. I lead a double existence: I get up very early in the mornings to write, and then I go to work as a secretary in a law firm. There, when I have nothing else to do, I read, concealing my book under the desk. My boss is nice, he just grins when he sees me at it. I've read the three long volumes of Proust in this way. The stories I write, by contrast, are short, only a few pages long; the events in them are bizarre, accidental, resisting interpretation. I don't want them to have any meaning. We all live in different places, separate from each other, but not as separated as we are from my father. To him it must appear that we've all gone as far away as possible, fleeing him.

*   *   *

When I married Daniel, my boyfriend from college, my parents saw each other again for the first time since their divorce. It was a small wedding, a tiny wedding: we had invited only our immediate family and one or two very close friends. For weeks in advance, I had dreaded this meeting of my parents. I had wanted to keep the wedding small because I didn't want the observant eyes of people on the outside to witness what to me seemed a raw, intimately painful event. I also wanted as few people as possible to *see* my father, I was so ashamed of him. It was as if we, my mother and Martin and I, were somehow exposed through him, our insides turned out on display.

Afterwards, in the restaurant, my father had stage fright: he had determined in his own mind that he ought to give a speech. I had no inkling of this intention of his until I noticed him scribbling furiously on his napkin. 'What are you doing?' I asked. He didn't hear me. I looked up and saw that he was muttering to himself with a little smile on his lips. Suddenly, abruptly, he commenced, with some brusque gesture to silence the other conversations at the table.

'What is it that brings two people together? As a biologist, I might bring the question down to a more basic level. I would reformulate it, I would ask, what brings any two organisms together, even such small organisms as microbes or single cells?' He rambled. He had no answer. There had been an idea, an inspiration, and it was as though he were grasping for it as it constantly eluded him. I felt mortified. Looking across the table, I saw Martin stiffen, staring at his salad. I couldn't see my mother's face. Daniel put his hand on my knee. My father went on and on, completely lost now, directionless. It seemed there was no way out of the maze into which he had wandered, until help came, miraculously, from the waitress, a buxom peroxide blonde who had a stronger German accent than he did.

'So – are vee ready to order yet? Haff you finished your speech?' she interrupted him cheerfully.

Everyone gaped. After a moment my father laughed good-naturedly and said, 'Yes, well, I guess I don't have anything more to say.'

Afterwards I learned that Daniel's family hadn't minded at all; they had found my father charming, likeable, his speech funny – although they didn't profess to understand it.

*

I feel a little sad, a little guilty, when I think of our wedding now. My father had wanted to 'give me away'. He had flown over from Germany by himself. He came the morning of the wedding carrying sixty red roses. But he had bought them from a vendor on the corner who was a drunk; and it ruined them for me to imagine how he must have fraternized with him, perhaps even sat next to him on the curb. In the courthouse, when we went before the judge, my father suddenly rose from his chair, thinking that now it was time, somehow, for him to give me away. But the judge motioned to him in no uncertain terms, flapping his hand, to sit down again. And so he did.

My father had brought it up beforehand, certainly, this idea of 'giving me away'; but I had waved it off with a laugh: 'It's not going to be that kind of wedding. No giving away.' I had tried to dismiss it in an offhand way that would not hurt his feelings, without saying straight out that the idea seemed preposterous to me. When the judge made that motion, as if my father were a schoolboy who had stood up out of turn, I felt a flash of smug satisfaction – 'That's how easy it is to put you in your place,' – similar to the almost triumphant satisfaction I felt later when the waitress, with her dyed hair and proudly displayed bosom, interrupted his speech.

But now, the thought of him standing up expectantly, having perhaps woken up early that morning with the same nervous butterflies in his stomach that he had on mornings before his lectures, having in fact made the entire trip in the anticipation of playing this fatherly role, only to be motioned by the pathetic judge to sit back down, now this thought burns me.

My parents were civil to each other during the whole event. Afterwards my mother said that although outwardly my father was recognizable, with the same mannerisms and habits of speech, she had felt an emptiness behind that. The man to whom she had been married for twenty-five years was no longer there. The figure posing as 'Christof' was someone else.

This idea of my father's *obliteration* has helped my mother come to terms with what happened.

*

My father stayed on for another week after the wedding, sleeping in his hotel and coming over to our apartment during the day. He frequently went out on his own 'for a little walk', and I guessed that he had found the bar a couple of blocks away, a run-down place with a green shamrock on its sign.

Once, when he was returning from his expedition, a neighbour in our apartment building was so startled by his approach that she slammed the front door in his face. In his white linen jacket and big sunglasses, my father must have seemed like a decadent apparition from another era, another planet.

25

THE THOUGHT OF my father is always at the bottom of my mind like something I've forgotten or neglected, unfinished business. There is a feeling of guilt attached to it, as if in turning my back to him, in being happy, I were committing some sort of betrayal.

My dreams let me know these things. My life has gone on, far away from him; my waking mind has sent him as far away as the moon, but in my sleep he is there, like the wood that I can't see for trees.

*

In the train station in Prague I watched a woman making her way to the bench across from where I was sitting. She put the plastic bag she was carrying down on the bench and then lowered herself with difficulty, bracing herself against the pillar. She sat not beside the bag, as I'd expected, but on it. She was skeletally thin, with hair like mine, wearing trousers and some kind of jacket and good quality sneakers, and she was filthy, her hands were black with dirt, even her face was blackened, her hair matted. She gazed blearily in my direction for a while and then slowly her head sank down until the chin touched her chest, and she stayed that way, her hands by her side, asleep. I couldn't take my eyes off her even though she didn't move and there was really nothing more to see. Other people might have given her a glance, sized her up, and then lost interest, but I kept on looking. I was fascinated by the fact that her bag actually functioned as a portable cushion, by this element of practical provision, of convenience, in what seemed on the surface an abandoned life. She carried the seat around with her for the purpose of sleeping more comfortably. I marvelled at her motionlessness in a position where most people would gradually slump and fall in one direction or another. She must have been perfectly balanced, for she did not so much as sway during the fifteen or twenty minutes that I sat across from her.

I stared at her, measuring the distance between us.

It is hard for me to imagine my future because I see my father there. Just because I can't, in a concrete way, imagine myself going the way he has gone, it frightens me all the more. I know that the pitfalls in each person's life are always in the blind spots, and the blind spots are always very close by, precisely so close that you cannot see them.

* * *

My father now goes to Collina, alone, once or twice a year. He keeps the same sheets on his bed from one visit to the next, eats food out of cans. He smokes cigarettes, which he puts out in an empty can. He drinks. When he feels lonely, he calls me or Martin long-distance across the Atlantic. He phones to say that it's beautiful in Collina, 'almost too beautiful,' and that he has decided he will never sell the house, that it's more important to him than anything else in life. Or else he phones to say that it's cold, it's been raining since the moment he arrived and he's spent the entire day sawing wood for the stove. He's just about sawed and burnt everything he can find, and the temperature has only gone up five degrees. 'Sometimes I hate Collina, I HATE this place, I honestly don't know why I come here.'

He is obsessed with the thought that he is alone and cut off from the world in that remote house. Once, soaking in a hot bath on a particularly chilly October day, he felt himself growing sleepier and sleepier, until he realized that he was slowly suffocating from the fumes of the gas heater that he had put on full-blast to warm the bathroom. *If I died here, no one would know.*

Sometimes he's drunk when he calls, sometimes he sounds sober. Sometimes I can't tell for sure.

I am haunted by the idea of him alone up there, in the silence. The last time I was in Collina I found signs of my father, traces of his presence. The remains of his last meal or meals were still stuck to the plastic tablecloth in the kitchen. On the windowsill in the bedroom upstairs there was a sardine can so tightly jammed with cigarette butts it made a mockery of the expression 'packed like sardines'. He must have stood at the window for hours, perhaps it was a rainy day, smoking cigarette after cigarette as he gazed into the distance. *I could drink in this beauty endlessly.*

His own room was like a tramp's lair. Opening the wardrobe I found unwashed clothes, heavy with his smell. I opened a drawer and made a mental register of the contents: champagne corks, wine cork, empty Coca-Cola bottle, empty plastic bags, unopened box of sucking candies flavoured caramel-mint. In a corner of the room, his telescope equipment: he had brought it with him, then never bothered to unpack it.

For a day or two, I became obsessed with imagining him there alone; reconstructing it. I found myself trying to experience things as though I were him.

*

When my father calls me long-distance from Collina I am always caught off-guard, violently startled: I am never prepared for my father's call.

*

Once he arrived at Collina late in the evening, tired from the long train journey; he was about to climb into his bed when he heard a delicate chirping noise. It seemed to come from his pillow. In the dim light of the single bulb hanging from a rafter in the centre of the room, he lifted the pillow and discovered underneath it a nest of newborn mice.

He carried them carefully outside, 'where I hoped the mother would find them.'

*

He telephones to tell me he is reading a novel he has found in the house, Flaubert's *Sentimental Education*. Was I the one who left it there? The cover of the book is encrusted, as he found everything when he arrived, with bat droppings. 'I had to get Silvana to come and clean.' In the *stalla* he discovered the corpse of a bat hanging from a rafter; instead of greyish or blackish it was snow-white. He thinks it must have been covered by some kind of white mould.

He calls to ask me when I am coming to Collina. He wants to spend time with me there. I don't even answer this.

'Doesn't the house mean anything to you?'

*

He phones to tell me he has 'the Collina Blues'.

*

One time when the phone rings we decide to let it go to the answering machine. It's my father, calling again from Collina. I could still pick it up, but something holds me back. My father is not used to answering machines. He doesn't have the knack of leaving messages, he is not used to speaking to an absence, an inanimate machine, a no-person at the other end. His voice falters, I can tell he feels exposed, naked. It is painful listening to him talk; but he continues, in a hesitant, entreating tone. And suddenly I have the eerie feeling that he knows I am here listening to him, hiding from him, eavesdropping. It's as if he were talking on in the hope of changing my mind and making me pick up the receiver after all. He is a powerful genie locked up in that little black box, cajoling me to let him out.

But I can't. I am afraid of him. I steel myself to be cruel.

26

A DREAM. My whole family – that is, my German aunts and uncles, my mother, Martin and I – are gathered for some kind of reunion or picnic. Only my father is missing. He is late, as usual. Characteristically, he is flouting punctuality. We wait and wait, and I am becoming extremely annoyed, because I know that he is late on purpose, in order to assert his freedom. When he finally arrives, he is dressed in women's clothes, in a long, frilly, lacy white dress of a hundred years ago. It is a surprise to us, but no one is very shocked or makes any comment. We all dismiss it as some sort of eccentric private joke, proceeding from my father's abstruse sense of humour, that less sophisticated minds cannot understand.

On waking I know that this dream was prompted by a remark of Martin's, that my father is looking more and more like my grandmother as he gets older.

*

My grandmother is not well, her state has been very slowly but steadily deteriorating. I have begun to call my father more frequently to have news of her. He tells me she can no longer leave her bed, barely recognizes her own children. He and my aunts now take turns visiting her at weekends. In addition to the nurses provided by the retirement home, they have hired a woman who keeps her company for a few hours every day. My grandmother's savings have already been eaten up by the expenses.

My aunts still are not speaking to each other. Hannelore cannot accept what is happening. Long after my grandmother has ceased to be mentally competent, after her brain has undergone, in my uncle Gerhard's words, 'a radical reduction', Hannelore still steadfastly maintains that the only thing wrong with her is nutrition: she isn't being fed properly. 'Obviously,' she has told my father, 'she is physically weakened and so her memory is a little weaker as well. But there is nothing wrong with her mind.' She reads nutritional books and copies out recipes for porridge and vitamin drinks. She sends them, written on odd, torn scraps of paper, to Erika; dispatches an endless stream of mail that drives Erika to tears.

*

When I was two years old, my parents went to Moscow together to attend a conference, leaving me in my grandmother's care. Although I have no memory of it, I know that the closeness I've felt to my grandmother all my life comes from this time that I spent with her. It was she who potty-trained me: there's a small photo album documenting the process, accomplished by means of a special wooden chair. The pictures were taken by my aunt Hannelore, who came to help my grandmother with the arduous task of taking care of me.

I've heard this story before; but now, on the telephone, my father tells me something that gives it an entirely new twist. Which is that my parents had planned to travel after the conference and come back after two weeks; but they were enjoying themselves so much that they extended their trip. By the time they got to Istanbul, they had been gone an entire month. My grandmother was desperate. She sent a telegram care of the consulate in Istanbul, begging them to return.

My mother has never mentioned this part either. My parents pretended not to have received the telegram, so that they could prolong their vacation still further. After taking in the sights of Istanbul, they continued on to Greece, visited Athens, lingered on some small island. Then a boat-ride across the straits of Otranto to Apulia, where they saw the unique *trulli* of Alberobello. Along the way they sent my grandmother postcards with brief, cheerful messages, knowing there was no way for her to respond. It was only after a full two months that they came back to reclaim me.

My father tells me about this abandonment of me without the slightest hint of apology or regret. I almost think I detect a note of childish pride over the escapade. Perhaps he thinks now that my grandmother has lost her memory, they have well and truly gotten away with it.

*

Opening the door to my grandmother's room on his last visit, my father thought that she was dead. The curtains were drawn, at four in the afternoon the room was in semi-darkness. 'She was lying motionless on the bed, her eyes closed, her hands by her sides, her lips white.'

Frightened, he ran to the nurses' station. The nurse told him, 'She's asleep, that's all. She's had her medicine already, so she won't be waking up again today.'

The next morning when he knocked at her door, my grandmother actually called out, 'Christof, come in.' – 'Of course,' he admits, 'the nurses had already been there, to freshen her up, as they put it, and they had told her I was coming.'

My father, who after leaving home wrote his mother a letter once a year, who 'forgot' to let her know of his marriage beforehand, this same man now comes once a month to sit by the side of his mother's bed for hours, making conversation which she may or may not comprehend. He strokes her forehead. At lunchtime he feeds her. 'First the soup, one little spoonful at a time, then the main course, one little forkful at a time, then the dessert. It takes for ever. It wears me down. Because she eats everything up, you know; her appetite is good.' He adds: 'But when I was a child she used to have to feed me too, and sometimes her patience wore thin as well. Yes, I think I can remember this – I would refuse to chew, and she always used to massage my cheeks to try to make me chew. So it's a kind of restitution if I have to feed her now . . .'

I feel there is a fake pathos in this idea of 'restitution', perhaps an implied message to me. In order not to let it resonate, I ask quickly, interrupting him, whether my grandmother is too weak to eat by herself.

'Yes, she is terribly weak. If you break up her bread into little pieces she can just manage to put them into her mouth by herself. But the heart is strong, the heart won't give up.'

My father tells me that she is given a nerve calmant to stop her constant agitated plucking at things, at herself, at her bandages, as well as opium to keep her intestines under control.

I sense that what my father wants is not an expression of feeling about my grandmother so much as recognition of *his* goodness, his loyalty, how he goes out of his way for her. I think: he has never been so good to his mother as now that she is dying, a doll-like body, as he himself describes her, all flesh gone from her bones, her skeleton covered only by the skin.

At the end of his visit she'd asked, 'When are you coming again?' He replied that he was coming in four weeks. 'What — in four weeks?' she exclaimed. Although she no longer had any concept of how long or short a time that was, the reaction, the disappointed, reproachful tone, was still ready upon recall.

I have just remembered something from my last visit with my grandmother: the wine bottles that I saw in her kitchenette, five or six of them, some empty, some full or half full. I had forgotten about them and now this memory has sprung up to disturb me. Did my father bring them there, did he drink with her, make her tipsy, my grandmother who was always self-possessed?

*

One time, to my surprise, my father himself picks up the phone. When I call it's always Silke who picks up, never my father. 'Just a minute,' he says, and then I hear him calling out to Silke, 'It *was* Irene.' He tells me that he decided to pick up the phone because he had a feeling it might be me. At the end of our conversation, he reminds me, 'I knew it was you.'

He tells me that Tut, the cat, died that afternoon. He has already dug a grave in the garden for him. Tut's dying, he says, was a terrible thing to watch. He tried to get out onto the balcony: he didn't have enough strength left to climb over the little ledge, but he somehow managed to *roll* over it. Next he tried to go down the stairs to the cellar. During the last hours of his life he kept dragging himself around the house 'as if trying to escape his fate.'

'How horrible,' I say, stricken by this image.

But my father, in a sudden change of tone, replies coolly, 'It's natural, the most natural thing in the world.'

*

Recently my grandmother has taken to counting, mumbling numbers to herself ceaselessly. No one knows what it is that she is counting.

One time my father found her lying with her knees drawn up under the blanket. She was fascinated by the mound made by her knees, was examining it, feeling its contours. And then she discovered, with a little laugh: 'That's me.'

It is when he tells me such anecdotes of my grandmother's dying, drily and without the slightest hint of emotion, that I feel I am glimpsing the tenderest, most compassionate side of his nature.

Everyone is saying that it would be good if my grandmother died, she can't want to live on like this; but my father doesn't accept this view. 'Who's to say if she's happy or unhappy? One can't know that.' It's almost as if he rejected the notion of unhappiness categorically, as if he were saying that such a thing doesn't exist, that even under apparent misery there may be a core of essential happiness, buried and private and bearing no relation to the perceptible conditions of an individual's life. I wonder if he is talking about himself.

*

I dream that my grandmother has died and I am in the living room of her house. In reality she has only lived in small apartments since I've known her, but in this dream there is a big house. My eye falls on a closed door and I decide to go through it. On the other side is another room that I've never

177

seen, in semi-darkness. There are more doors and I select one and go through it into the next room, and from this on to another, and another. There are little stairways leading up and then down, further rooms glimpsed off to the side. All is still, deserted, the windows closed. The furnishing is old-fashioned, with carpets, paintings, in one room there is a grand piano. I hurry on with a feeling of suppressed excitement, opening doors, shutting them. No one knows about these rooms, or else they have been forgotten and I am the first to rediscover them. I have a thought at the back of my mind that here is a place for me. Here are many places in which I could hide away and live.

*

When I think of my grandmother now it's not so much her person I think of as her aura, the feeling I had around her. It has something to do with the deep hush of her apartment in Munich after our excursions into the hot and noisy city, or the delicate clinking of her white porcelain cups when we stirred powdered cocoa into our milk at breakfast. I associate with her an atmosphere of peacefulness that for all I know may have been quite at odds with her personality. There were our rituals that stayed the same throughout the years, such as the exchange of gifts, the little presents my mother helped my brother and me make for her at birthdays and Christmas, and the chocolate bars she never forgot to hand us at the end of our visits, with five-mark coins taped to the back of them. When I left home I felt her as a sort of faraway anchor, a permanent presence in my otherwise uncertain, vagabond life. I'd write her the occasional dutiful letter, and there would always be something a little surprising about her response, something more specific, more personal than I'd expected. She asked me to send her something I'd written; but I never did.

*

I dream that I am attending my grandmother's funeral and I am wearing a black suit. In real life I don't own a black suit. But the suit in my dream is a specific one, it's the tuxedo from Chile that was my great-uncle Hermann's legacy, passed down to my father, to my aunt Erika, and now to me.

In real life, I won't be attending my grandmother's funeral; America is too far away.

27

I AM SITTING IN a darkened theatre, a vast, immense auditorium, full of people. The rows of seats fan out and upward from the screen or stage, which is so far away that I have no idea what the spectacle is that everyone has come to watch. I must have come late, slipping in quietly through an entrance at the back and sitting in one of the last rows so as not to disturb anyone. There is little light: it is nearly pitch-black where I am sitting. All at once I notice that my father has come in through the entrance behind me and is standing in the aisle just to my left. Staring straight ahead, he says loudly: *'Dann werde ich nicht traurig sein, daß es für mich keine Bedeutung gab.'*

I am petrified, I don't call out to him as he starts walking down the aisle. I realize that he can't see all the people around him because his vision is not yet adjusted to the darkness. *Then I won't be sad that there was no meaning for me.* His words sound plaintive, he's like a child in a dark room, talking loudly to quell its fear, consoling itself for having been left out in the distribution of something nice that all the other children have been given.

The second part of the sentence is less important than the

first; the word 'meaning' itself has no weight, it seems a mere placeholder, that could just as well be substituted by other words. It's the phrase *I won't be sad* that is laden with significance. My father's voice has a truculent overtone that strikes terror in my heart. It implies a threat. I am as afraid of him as if he had come into the theatre carrying a weapon, intending to murder us all.

This dream depicts my father's loneliness as I imagine it. It's not the loneliness of someone who has been left alone by the others, so much as that of someone who has always wanted to be left alone, who hugs his solitude fiercely to himself.

✵

My father calls me on the telephone. When I ask him how he's doing and he replies, 'Oh, well, not bad, not bad,' I get the clear impression that the opposite is true.

✵

Martin gives my father tartan flannel pyjamas for Christmas and I give him a dressing-gown in a different tartan. In retrospect I am disturbed by the idea that we are dressing him from head to toe, that we're making a clown of him with this outfit of which everything is a little too big, those American lumberjack sizes, all in clashing checks. But that wasn't our intention, rather our collaboration in gifts has sprung up out of a need for mutual reassurance, strength in numbers, for solidarity vis-à-vis our father.

✵

My brother, Daniel and I spend Christmas at my mother's house. About a month later I learn that my father spent the time between Christmas and New Year's Eve in hospital. He says he had a bacterial stomach infection. Somehow I don't believe him. I don't know what to believe. The hospital where he stayed is right across from my old school: for nine years I saw it every day, I even went inside a few times when my best friend had broken her wrist in gym class; but now, try as I may, I can't summon a picture of it in my mind. I draw a blank.

*

For my birthday my father gives me a beautiful Pelikan fountain pen, a 1930s model. He says it's the same as a pen that his father gave him when he was a boy. 'It meant a lot to me.' A year ago he gave Martin an identical pen, but without mentioning this story. I suspect that he's made it up. But I don't know if that makes it meaningless or even more poignant.

*

I write my father a letter responding to his request that I spend time with him in Collina. Rather than refuse outright I execute a kind of song and dance that is intended to distract him from the no that is hidden in its midst, between the lines. As I write it I feel that it is a witty letter, or at least a charming one. I compose it with a kind of humming glee. My style in German is arch and fancy because the language no longer comes naturally to me. I feel that I am throwing out words like salt and pepper to blind my father, that he will read the letter without realizing what it says.

Some kind of doubt makes me hold the letter back, I keep it to reread the following morning. But even then I can find no fault with it and I send it off.

It's happened to me so many times before: the moment the

envelope disappears into the chute it's as though I were cured from a temporary insanity. Immediately I see the letter clearly for what it is. I recognize in my own dishonesty a cheap righteousness masquerading as innocence; and at the same time a cowardice and weakness vis-à-vis my father that disgusts me. It's like that image I was shown in school as a child, *Schöne Frau–Hässliche Alte*, that depicted a beautiful woman or an ugly old witch depending on how you focused. My image of myself has suddenly wobbled.

*

Dreams about my father are coming to me more and more often. I wish I could stop them. In one dream I am shouting at him. He has at first on his face that complacent, superior, amused expression, but I am shouting with all my strength: 'You pretend it means nothing to you, you pretend to be above it all, but I know you're lying. You cling to that title of yours, *Herr Professor*, like a life-raft, and now it's all you have left.' I don't remember exactly what other things I say, but my whole anger is coming out. I am telling him off, something I've never done in real life. And as I am shouting at him I watch him become slowly transformed, his ironic smile disappears, his face sags. By the time I fall silent he is only a small, helpless old man.

In another dream I see my father sitting by himself, withdrawn, scribbling furiously on some large sheets of paper, tears rolling down his face. There are figures, calculations of money, as well as words and parts of sentences followed by multiple exclamation marks. He is making his case, continuing to marshal arguments before an absent court.

I approach him from behind – I am invisible, a ghost –

and put my hand on his head the way I might do to a child whose head is small enough to fit in my palm. It is a private gesture of tenderness; he can't perceive my disembodied presence.

*

Phoning me one day across the Atlantic, my father begins our conversation with this ominous phrase: '*I want something from you.*' He pauses as if awaiting my response. For a moment my heart is in my mouth. My first, confused thought is that I must refuse it, whatever it is. What has he come to demand? What debt is he calling in?

It turns out to be a perfectly reasonable request: he merely wants me to translate some short business letters into Italian. I try not to let my relief show as I agree to do it. Afterwards I am still disturbed by the way he said that: *I want something from you.* It's almost as if he'd been trying out the sound of it, testing its effectiveness for some indefinite future use.

I'm in training for that day, when it comes. I'm preparing myself, steeling myself, strengthening myself to say no.

This is my most secret fear: Silke leaves my father and he shows up on our doorstep, asking to be let in. I have no choice, he has no place else to go. He installs himself in a back room and lives on and on there, like some monstrous creature with enormous needs and appetites, ruling our lives tyrannically through his inability to take care of himself.

For the first time in my life I am afraid of my father's anger. I can't really picture it, he used to be angry so rarely, and even then one could not take it seriously. But I know instinctively what it will be like: a coldness colder than dry ice, a wind blowing away all his sentimentality like flimsy clouds.

His voice on the telephone sounded to me like the voice of someone speaking from a deep pit.

This conception has sprung up spontaneously: an immense reservoir of wrath in the place where my father used to be.

*

And then again I remember this. One evening, it was shortly before I was supposed to go off to college in America, something had come over me and I was in my room, face down on my bed, crying, bawling in complete desperation. Of all people it was my father who came to comfort me. He sat down on the side of my bed and talked to me, and it was nothing he said that eventually calmed me down, so much as the feeling that my fear of life, my terror of absolutely everything, was something he could understand better than anyone else.

*

Sometimes I think that writing about my father is an act of aggression, that I am doing him a kind of violence. Then again at other times I want him to read what I have written, as if this could change something.

I regret never having attended one of his lectures. What was he like, as a teacher? How did his students see him? I was always secretly afraid that they mocked him, that he was a laughing-stock. How happy, how relieved I was when I heard, from a classmate whose sister was studying biology, that he was one of the most popular professors.

I rehearse the events of his life: childhood in Danzig, the flight, studies in Tübingen, coming to America and marriage to my mother. Because I've heard these few stories more than once, like landmarks that keep reappearing, I have the illusion that I know it all, that the whole map is *terra cognita*. But of course in reality I am merely treading the same paths over and over in the midst of a vast unknown country.

In the course of writing it seems that my father has been receding from me even more, like a face that was so clear in a dream and has dissipated on waking, eluding my grasp.

28

COLLINA, JUNE 1996

My father has phoned from Florence to let me know which train he will be on. I have come to the station of Pontecchio well in advance. The little station building is empty, the ticket window closed. I go out through the back and sit on one of the two green benches facing the tracks. The sun is already quite low, but the yellow-painted wall at my back is giving off some of the heat it has absorbed during the day. Across the track there is a concrete wall and on top of that a high dusty hedge shielding the houses behind it. The place has a surreal emptiness about it, like a painting by de Chirico. My stomach is knotted.

We are going to spend two weeks in Collina, just the two of us. Daniel offered to come with me but I said it was OK, I could come alone. My father is joining me from Silke's villa in Provence, where they have been vacationing. He is three days late. On the evening of the day he had originally planned to leave, he called to say that he had decided to stay another day.

'The mistral is blowing so incredibly today. The sky is

ndous,' was the reason he gave. 'Besides, we're going to a
al restaurant tonight, a converted train station on a railway
line that is now defunct. It was recommended by none other
than Horst Bickler, the food critic of *Zeit Magazin*.'

After this I had two additional days of reprieve because my
father and Silke were taken terribly ill, with vomiting and
diarrhoea.

'But the mussels we ate in the restaurant recommended by
Horst Bickler of *Zeit Magazin* were so unbelievably delicate that
one wouldn't want to attribute this to them,' said my father
with good-humoured irony when he called me the next time.

By chance I found an old issue of *Zeit Magazin* lying on the
kitchen counter. It contained a photograph of this expert, who
appeared to be about the same age as my father and of a
similar complexion, though bearded and with glasses.

It seemed that my father was a little afraid of making the
journey alone. It was too long, or rather the train connections
were too bad, for him to make it all in one day.

'I'll spend the night in Genoa,' he said gamely. 'I'll eat
bouillabaisse on the pier. – I'm sure I'll be able to find some sort
of hotel, even without advance reservations.' I had the distinct
impression that he was worried about the whole thing.

A metal bell starts clanging above my head, announcing the
train's approach. I stand up and walk down the platform. The
train pulls in; people pour out of the doors, workers returning
home from their jobs in the city. They come in clusters, like
seeds spilling out of pods. I've been turning left and right so
as to scan the three cars of the train at once; but my father
was in the very rear and I miss the moment when he steps
down onto the platform, the last to get off.

He is loaded down, with a heavy suitcase in one hand and
a microscope case in the other, his large square shoulder bag

slung around his neck. There is something unaccustomed and pitiful in seeing him struggle across the platform with his luggage. I feel a pang. He looks surprisingly small to me – as if I had expected him to be larger than life.

As I embrace my father I see, over his shoulder, some people in the train looking down at us smiling, touched: what a nice scene. The daughter greeting her father.

'It's so wonderful to be picked up! Thank you, thank you so much!'

Though bleary from the alcoholic refreshments he's had along the way, my father is at the same time buoyed by the adventure of his stay in Genoa.

'It's an incredible story. But I can't tell you now. No, it's too good to tell quickly! You'll have to be patient.'

*

Next morning, I am on my second cup of coffee when my father comes downstairs. He looks refreshed. 'I feel refreshed,' he says. He says he woke up at the crack of dawn but then was able to go back to sleep again. 'And then I had a big, wonderful bath. But don't let me disturb you,' he adds. 'Keep writing, we'll have plenty of time to talk later.'

When we sit in silence on the terrace, I become more aware of the noises around us: different flies, a higher-pitched plaintive vibrato that lingers in one place, almost like a mosquito; then the medium-pitched buzzes that zoom purposefully here and there, growing higher or lower as a measure of distance; occasionally the deep drone of a heavy bumble-bee. On the field below the road Giorgio and his son are working with the tractor and every once in a while we hear Giorgio's cry – *Alloraa!*

Yesterday, I had taken my father's suitcase and started

walking with it toward the car when he stopped me. 'No! First I want to have an ice cream at the bar!' For some reason this small manifestation of wilfulness on his part unbalanced me; I was actually upset, as if I'd wanted to control and repress him the way I control and repress my memories.

Today, everything seems easier, and I think to myself: it's not so bad after all.

*

In the evening, when we are again sitting on the terrace after dinner, by the light of the little lantern, he finally relents and tells me the story of his night in Genoa. As he tells it it's difficult to follow, rambling, full of divergent ideas, climaxes piled one on top of the other, innumerable details each lovingly burnished but scattered randomly, like metal shavings without the magnetic force to bring them into alignment. Only at the very end, taking a step back, am I able to see the shape of the whole.

He had arrived in Genoa, alone in a foreign city, without advance reservations. 'Of course I didn't even know where I was going to sleep that night.' He was a little frightened and at the same time a little exhilarated.

'It reminded me of the time I first came to America as a student, when I landed in New York and had to find a hotel . . .'

I see him going to the station bar and ordering a glass of *spumante* and a *bombolone*: feeling reassured because he knows the words for these things. It also gives him confidence that he has noticed a Tourist Information office on his way to the bar: thus one thing is leading smoothly to another. He orders a second glass of *spumante*.

The girl in the Tourist Information office seemed bored, glad for a customer. He told her he wanted a room that was 'nice, quiet, and inexpensive'. After leafing in her binder for a moment, the girl proposed a room so cheap it could only be the lowest sort of dive. Apparently, in sizing him up, she had decided that 'inexpensive' was the operative word. Well, how should she know he was *Herr Professor*? My father archly, but without bearing a grudge, corrected her impression by saying that he was willing to pay three times that amount and he wanted a *nice* room, with a private bath.

The mistake is significant, a harbinger of things to come. My father is experiencing the full meaning of anonymity. The connection between his identity, who he has been throughout his life, and his present physical person, as he might be observed from a window, walking through the narrow streets, has suddenly become loosed, almost arbitrary. It is up to him to hold the two together – otherwise they could float apart.

'My hotel was in a nice part of town. It must have been the blacksmiths' quarter at one time – all the street names seemed to have to do with iron, hammers, and nails.'

A vague delusion of escape quickens his step.

He checked in, washed, then went out again in search of dinner. He was picky in selecting a restaurant. The first one he passed was too touristy, the second too expensive. As in fairy tales, the third restaurant was perfect. It was called simply *Da Alberto*, and a handwritten menu was posted in the window. My father stood there poring over it for a long time. It was still a little early, and when he finally went inside, he was the first customer. He chose a corner table. The waitress, a young girl with a brisk, but shy air, greeted him and gave him the menu.

'She was so pretty and quick. I guessed at once she was the daughter of the owner.'

My father asked for '*soppa di pesce*' and white wine. The girl said she had to go ask her father if they had *zuppa di pesce* that night. She came back from the kitchen and said that they did not, but that he could have *zuppa di cozze* instead.

My father did not know what *cozze* were: but the word, by its exact resemblance to the German *Kotze*, reminded him too graphically of his stomach illness of the preceding days; and so he ordered salmon cooked in champagne instead.

There follows now a long series of exchanges. He wants *zuppa di cozze* after all (once he's realized it means mussels), in addition to the salmon; wants another carafe of wine; wants to compliment the chef on the salmon, which is the best he's ever eaten. On one level these are all simply excuses to call the waitress to his table. He has established a relationship with her that he is working to develop. Instinctively she invokes her father – 'I'll go and ask my father' – as a protection against this odd man. And that adds to his pleasure because he has thus established a line of communication with the inner sanctum of the kitchen, the invisible power behind the façade, with the chef himself. Soon the girl is secondary, a mere go-between, carrying messages back and forth between him and the chef.

'The mussels themselves were somewhat puny. But the sauce was divine. I slurped it using a shell – like this. And the salmon: it was *so* exquisite that I asked the waitress if I could have a copy of the menu to take with me. She seemed a little taken aback, but she said she would ask her father.'

All of these things – the food, the wine, the suspense of the human triangle he has created – combine to a heightened, thrilling enjoyment of the moment. It is in this ecstatic mood that he perceives a large group of people who have just come into the restaurant. They are all young, in their twenties and thirties, and, it seems to him, almost excessively good-looking. They commandeer tables; indeed they seem to take over the restaurant, to make it their space. Even though it has become quite crowded, they act unaware of anyone around them. The men are so handsome, the women so beautiful, all of them so well dressed: 'I thought immediately, they must be actors and actresses, they could only belong to the world of the theatre.'

My father watches them – he has finished eating and is slowly drinking his wine – spellbound with fascination. They have moved several tables together to form one long one; carafes of wine and glasses and water pitchers have appeared as if by pre-arrangement. A pale, slightly heavy-set man with raven-black hair negotiates with the waitress over their order, which they are making as a group. They are laughing and talking, the Italian cadences sound almost like opera, emphatic and self-assured. Here and there my father seems to recognize a word or a phrase and he tries to hold on to it, to capture it; he feels he is very close to remembering its meaning, until a woman's laughter, rising suddenly above the rest, erases it.

'They were all playing roles: there was the pensive, melancholy type; the show-off; the ladies' man; the clown. Among the women there was the somewhat older, experienced belle, courted by everyone; and on the other hand the coy ingénue . . .'

Because they are so beautiful he concludes that they cannot be real. This whole, rich pageant is theatre, and he is the privileged spirit for whose benefit it is being enacted. At once he is surrounded by a fabulous world in which everything is not what it seems, a world that glows with the gilt and glamour and mystery of artifice, of art. And he, too, is a participant in the world of actors: no one knows him, he has left his identity behind.

I see him sitting there by himself in his crumpled white linen jacket, surveying the scene from his vantage apart, his glasses slightly crooked on his face. He has lit up a cigarette.

Certainly more than once there is a curious glance in his direction – the woman in the red blouse has caught his eye several times; and hasn't the young one, the ingénue, just whispered something about him to the man with the beret which has caused the latter to turn his head quickly in his direction? He senses that he presents an enigma; perhaps he himself is the most interesting, mysterious character of all.

Suddenly he has an idea. It is more difficult now to get the attention of the waitress. Her movements seem to have become speeded up as in old movies as she rushes back and forth, carrying dishes and writing down new orders; but these movements are still neat and precise, a sort of brisk staccato amidst the hazy warm blur of voices and laughter and delicious smells that the restaurant has become. Nonetheless he manages to hail her over to his table by holding his index finger raised, a gesture he sometimes uses in his lectures to signify that he is about to make a fairly momentous point.

'Ah! *Prego!* I'm sorry to disturb you. It won't take long. I just wanted to ask one question. Just one question. These people over there, they must surely be from the *Festivale di Genova?*'

'Oh,' says the waitress, taken aback. 'I don't know. I'll have to ask my father.'

The girl never did come back with an answer; maybe because the *Festivale di Genova* was a pure invention of my father's. The idea came to him because he had recently been in Avignon, where the summer festival had been going on. But the more he thinks about it the more probable it seems to him that such a festival *should* exist. It's a compelling postulate. Isn't it almost inevitable? After all, these people, so beautiful, so out of the ordinary, these actors and actresses – what else could have brought them together but a festival? And in a town like Genoa, a seaside town, how could there *not* be, in the summer, some sort of festival?

In Avignon they have *bouillabaisse*, here it is *zuppa di pesce*; the *moules* of Southern France are the *cozze* of Northern Italy – the poisonous effects of the former reappearing, by a mystical transmutation, in the name of the latter. Everywhere things are the same, there is an underlying equivalence to all reality: it is merely a question of translation. This insight appears to him all at once so solid, so shining, so true, that it gives him a feeling of triumph and power. It's almost as if he had invented, not just the *Festivale di Genova*, but the entire scene around him in all its richness and color.

As he sits there laughing to himself, the waitress comes and brings him his bill. He looks at it, reaching for his wallet. And then he notices that the figures don't add up.

'I looked at the bill. I looked again. It was only a fifth of what I had figured out it should be!'

He couldn't pay this, he told the waitress: it was too little. Finally the chef himself made his appearance. My father complimented him profusely, then pointed out the mistake on the bill. Could this be right? Yes, yes, it was right, replied the chef.

'But it doesn't add up, all that I've eaten – and the wine . . .'

'*Signore*,' the chef then said to him, 'the mathematics are *my* mathematics, and they are right.' And he personally presented my father with the copy of the menu he had requested earlier.

The metamorphosis was complete. My father had been mistaken for a food critic.

My father was delighted by his luck in having eaten such a good meal in such a charming place and not having had to pay for it. 'But I didn't lie,' he protested, chuckling. 'And I intend to send the menu to Horst Bickler. I think he should know about this place.'

*

After the first few days we have established a routine. When my father comes out of his room in the morning, I join him briefly for a second cup of coffee, then I go back upstairs to read or write. Neither of us are using our old rooms: I have taken the little room that used to be my parents', because it has the morning sun; while my father is using my brother's old room. I close the door and sit at the little wooden table by the window, where I can look out toward Gino and Silvana's house, observe the activity on their field.

I go downstairs again sometime between eleven and twelve; he meanwhile has done the dishes from last night's dinner. He insists on taking over this chore: he doesn't want to be 'useless'. There is always a slight awkwardness when we first sit down together. We don't know how to talk to each other. Usually I am the one who gets hungry first and suggests lunch. We prepare the meal together, carrying the table outside onto the terrace, putting out the cheese and cold meats, the bread and some salad. I have the feeling we are both making a conscious effort; there's a sense of well-intentioned exertion beneath our leisurely activity.

No sooner have we begun eating than the wasps are upon us, hovering around the table, impossible to shoo away. There are more than usual this year; there must be a nest somewhere close by. They settle on our plates, our food: there's a danger of swallowing one by accident. One time a wasp attaches itself to a piece of salami and I threaten it with the blade of my knife. How close do I have to come before it gets the message? I end up cutting it in half. I throw the carcass onto the ground where, afterwards, with a delayed shock at my own cruelty, I see ants tugging at it, two different factions pulling in opposite directions.

In the afternoon, when my father and I sit on the terrace reading, I notice our similarity, how after concentrating on our books for a few minutes we will both look out into the valley and get lost in daydreaming.

*

My father is reading *Humboldt's Gift*. The book was given to him years ago, he thinks, by my mother, who loves Saul Bellow's works. 'It's been lying around all these years and now I happened to see it and decided to bring it along.'

He has never read anything by Saul Bellow before, but he thinks this is wonderful, 'a great American novel'. He sits at the kitchen table, chuckling over it. 'I *identify* with these people. This is unbelievable . . . terrible!' And he recounts to me the succession of awful things that are happening to the protagonist.

My father always imagines or tries to imagine the process by which a book was written. He can't simply be a reader, he tells me; he has to imagine himself as the author. How did the author get his ideas?

Reading, with those little rimless oval reading glasses, my father has the air of a slow student, trying overly hard to concentrate, breathing audibly with the effort, the way students look who are studying for an exam they know they will fail. He stops often, to light a cigarette, pour himself a little wine.

'In these pages the author seems to have lost interest in his own story, it seems a bit laboured here,' he notes with satisfaction. 'No one can have ideas all the time, not even Saul Bellow. Perhaps he had writer's block. Do you ever have writer's block?' He sees me writing in my diary.

'Of course,' I say lightly. 'It happens all the time. I sit down and have nothing to say.'

'Come on, that can't be true,' he says. And jokingly, 'Write about me.'

'Hm, that's an interesting idea, maybe I will!' I keep up the same bantering tone. 'But then I'll really have to see that piece of paper you hid from me earlier.' He had pulled a sheet of paper out of a folder which he said was his 'diary' from the last time he'd been here. '*I hate Collina. For darkness reigns...*' After reading the first few words he quickly tucked it away, saying it was 'too silly'.

'No, no, on second thoughts...' He laughs, but uneasily, as if he sensed the half-seriousness behind my pressing.

*

I put on a straw hat and my father looks at me and says: 'You are still exactly the same as twenty years ago.'

My father wants to eat veal kidneys. We buy them at the supermarket and consult one of my mother's recipe books for their preparation. It's quite elaborate: they have to be pre-fried in butter, then rolled in salt, pepper, and parsley and let sit for a couple of hours. Only then are they cooked, in fresh butter to which olive oil and garlic have been added. 'It's an adventure,' my father says. 'We'll see what happens.' As we prepare them together I feel that we are contriving this moment to become a memory, a sentimental memory of something shared; it is being framed before it is even done. Of course I won't eat the kidneys (my father wants to have them rare): I make myself a piece of chicken instead.

*

In a moment of frustration at myself I cry out, 'I do *everything* wrong!'

My father looks at me with an expression of amused surprise. 'Now you've finally made it well again.'

'What are you talking about?'

'When you were little, you once said, "Papi does *everything* wrong." Now you've made up for that.'

My father's memory of me as a small child is of how difficult I was, how stubborn, how I used to scream piercingly, on and on. Once on a walk I wanted to go in a different direction from the one we were going and he had to pick me up and carry me home, crying and screaming the whole way. People stared at us. They thought perhaps he was beating me.

*

Just before falling asleep I have a very vivid, sensory memory of our old apartment in Germany. It's more a memory of a feeling, of a moment in which nothing happened; but it allows me to reconstruct certain visual details I'd forgotten, like the greyish linoleum floor in the hallway.

And then I remember these things: how in the summer the two of us used to get up early, at 5.30, and bicycle down to the lake for a swim before school and work. The water was icy, smelling of algae, its unruffled surface silver and opalescent in the dawn light. There was no sound but our own quiet splashing. It was so beautiful it made me want to shout. Before going into the water my father produced two minty-tasting disinfectant tablets; we each put one in our mouths and sucked on them as we swam so that we wouldn't catch cold.

Or how, when I couldn't sleep or woke up again late at night, sometimes there would be a light in the living room and I'd see that my father was still awake. I'd go out and whine a little and he would give me *Zuckerwasser*, water mixed with a bit of sugar, to make me go back to sleep again. He said that was what he had been given as a little boy. The solemnity with which he prepared this drink, stirring the sugar round and round with a spoon, reassured me so much that as far as I can recall, it really did always work.

＊

'It's really ugly to get old.' We have walked up the hill to the house, and my father had to stop every ten paces – he seemed to be counting them, to be setting himself this goal – to catch his breath. When we reach the house he sits, breathing heavily, in the armchair in the living room. For a moment I worry that he might have a heart attack. He says he remembers how in the past he used to come up the hill with two heavy suitcases, then go back down for more. I make a sorrowful face at first, but then decide to turn it to a joke. I say, 'You could always start going to *Fit und Fun* with Silke.'

＊

Everyone in the town smiles at him. We go to have the car repaired and the mechanic doesn't even want to accept payment. My father hands him ten thousand lire: the mechanic acts as if it were just too much kindness, as if my father's visit alone had delighted him enough.

The peasants who live near Collina used to regard my father with awe, ever since one of them happened to see a German television documentary about science in which he made a brief appearance. My father was always tickled by the irony that he had been filmed standing with a piece of high-tech equipment that he had no idea how to use. Now I sense a new element in their attitude toward him. There is a knowing look in their eyes.

I tell my father I don't like Greci, a local man whose friendliness is transparently phoney and cloying. '*Like? Like?*' my father says with a puzzled air, as if 'liking' were an irrelevant and remarkably un-useful concept; or as if it would never have occurred to him to waste a thought on Greci. 'I don't know – he just *exists*.'

*

My father says: 'Thank you for these beautiful days. I don't remember the last time I've felt so happy in Collina.'

The last time he was alone here, he says, he had a terrible stomach virus. It came upon him suddenly, while he was shopping in Pontecchio. 'It just exploded,' he tells me, although I don't really want to know. 'I'll spare you the details.' But then, later, he can't resist telling me one or two details: how he had to run into the nearest bar; the toilet was one of those holes in the floor, over which you have to crouch in the most impossible position; then he had to race back up to the house. For over a week, he only went back and forth between his bed and the toilet. 'The worst part was, I couldn't even eat anything, even milk was rejected immediately by my stomach.' It was only when he had started to recover that he was able to make the briefest trip down to buy medication.

He is afraid of the same thing happening again. Maybe it's just his imagination, but he thinks the symptoms are beginning again. We go to the pharmacy, where he requests loudly, unembarrassed in front of other customers: 'A *strong* remedy against diarrhoea.' When the woman asks, 'Is it for an adult?' he asserts, just as boldly: 'It's for me.'

Under the pretext of wanting to replace the 'bad bacilli' in his stomach with good ones, he is eating yogurt and ricotta and cheese. I remember reading that milk products help the liver to regenerate. At the grocery store my father has bought *Kyr*, a yogurt-like product containing *streptococcus thermophilus, lactobacillus bulgaricus, lactobacillus acidophilus,* and *bifidobacterium.* 'This is what makes the Bulgars live for ever,' he says. And he's been spooning it greedily out of the little plastic containers as if it were really the elixir of longevity.

I ask him, tentatively, if anything ever came of those experiments about *apoptosis.* He just waves my question off: he doesn't want to talk about it.

He seems to be holding back, drinking moderately at meal-times, but I know he squirrels bottles away in his room. He goes on little furtive errands, up and down the stairs, there are sudden unexplained absences, all wrapped in an air of subterfuge which irritates me.

I am thrown back into my old compulsion of watching him, fearfully interpreting everything he does. I am in a state of constant uncertainty and suspense, ready to react to any change in him; whereas he seems comparatively relaxed. He'll look at me sometimes as if amused and pleased by my existence, as if I belonged to some strange but loveable tribe encountered in the jungle.

The smell of my father's toothpaste lingering in the bathroom after he has gone to bed reminds me of my grandmother. But of course it's simply the most common German brand, millions of Germans use it. Last night I got up to go to the bathroom and although there was no light in his room a stench of cigarette smoke was seeping through the cracks in his door.

The things that I hate about myself when I am with him: my tendency to be complaisant, to cater to his moods, to be submissive in a fundamental way. I play exactly the womanly role that he has always got from the women in his life, from his mother and my mother and from Silke. I can't help myself. He for his part often calls me 'Erika' or 'Silke' by mistake.

One time, in order to be alone I go upstairs to practise my flute. I've taken it up again here, just a bit. He follows me after a while to say that my playing is beautiful, it's making him feel so much better. 'Don't stop yet, play a little longer.' And something in me warms to this role of nurse and good fairy, to the idea that my playing is soothing and helping him. I can't resist it. The next moment I feel manipulated and harden myself against him.

*

As we walk through the square in Pontecchio, my father says, 'Illness is wonderful, because you feel reborn when you get well again.'

He hates the little supermarket where I like to shop, and insists on taking me to his favourite place, 'Signora Angelini's'. The combination bar-grocery store is run by a couple, but he likes to refer only to the wife, a pretty woman with rich brown curls, red lipstick, flashing eyes.

'Oh – you've come back! Did you just arrive? How can I help you?'

My father gets royal treatment. And even though we need little, he wants to buy everything, to make a big, generous *spesa*. I am increasingly mortified as he makes a production of ordering large amounts of everything he can think of, especially the most expensive items, pretending to consult me when he has already made up his own mind. He speaks to me loudly in German and I feel he is shouting. He is playing the *grande signore*, for whom ordering half a pound of *prosciutto toscano* is simply an expression of *joie de vivre*; he might as well throw it out the window later, so little does any thought of eating it enter into the act. He likes opening his wallet, looking through the thick multi-coloured stack of notes with a mien of incomprehension — what is what? — pulling out finally one of the largest and handing it to Signora Angelini as if it were play money to him. Then comes the best part, when Signora Angelini commands her daughter to offer us drinks.

I decline, am pressed, finally say *acqua minerale* — 'in typical Irenesque fashion,' my father comments later, sarcastically. (My narrow-minded priggishness, my ungenerous aloofness.) He for his part accepts gladly an *aperitivo della casa*, mixed by Signora Angelini herself out of five different ingredients, a huge glass. A man sitting at the bar gets up from his seat and offers it to my father. My father takes the seat, then gets up again and proclaims something about paying for his drink, full well knowing it's on the house.

'No, no, please,' says Signora Angelini graciously.

And now the situation really begins to get a little unfortunate. Another man who was just about to pay for his glass of wine says, 'Then I won't pay either.' Signora Angelini blushes. 'Then nobody pays, go on.' She is clearly joking, but the man insists, wanting to be taken seriously: 'If they don't pay, then I shouldn't have to pay either!'

'But they don't come as often.'

'Exactly, I'm such a good customer, you should give *me* special treatment . . .'

My father emerges from the bar in a rapturous mood. 'I *love* Pontecchio!' I can tell the difference the drink has made in his voice. We walk across Piazza della Repubblica and he embraces it all: the late afternoon sunshine on the pale stuccoed arcades, Renato's newspaper shop, the friendliness of all these simple people, who love him.

When we come home I decide to take a bath, and as I sit in the little tub looking out at the sky inundated with gold, letting the weak trickle of warm water run over my skin, I suddenly start crying. There's no real reason except tiredness, exhaustion from being with him.

*

After dinner, we see fireflies and he tells me about a watch he had when he was small, that had the numerals painted in radium. 'Later,' he says, 'they stopped making these watches, because the women employed to paint the numerals all died of cancer.' He used to lie under the covers in the dark and look at this watch for minutes on end through a magnifying glass.

'I could actually see individual flashes of light. I couldn't get over it – to think that each flash of light was a single atom decaying, that I could actually *see* this!'

My father never used to talk much about his childhood; now, in the evenings, he's begun to bring up some things he remembers, narrating them in a quiet way, holding them at a distance with a little laugh.

He tells me about a prank in which he took part when he was in school in Danzig. 'I'm still ashamed of it today.' It was usual at the time to write exercises on slate tablets with chalk pencils. While the German students came equipped with a fresh set of pencils at the beginning of each school year, which they carried in nice leather cases and thoughtlessly discarded when half used, the Polish students had only one or two pencils; they had to sharpen them sparingly and use them down to the smallest stub. 'One afternoon, I joined a group of boys; we went through the desks of an empty classroom taking all these collections of little stubs that they had; and we threw them out the window, just for the hell of it.'

*

Another night he tells me about his first trip to America. He was very young, not much more than twenty. The Roswell Park Cancer Center in Chicago had invited him to speak because, 'at that time, my research was world-famous. I was world-famous.' His teacher had spread the word about his work and its promise for the cure of cancer. He remembers how he walked out of the train station in Chicago, and down the street with his little suitcase, and into the first hotel, where an overnight cost fifty cents. The manager at the front desk took his fifty cents and said to him, 'I'm sure you will find it clean and safe.' He climbed the stairs and found that the hotel consisted of an enormous space subdivided by partitions into little cubicles with cots. He realized it was a hotel for derelicts, a doss-house. The partitions didn't reach all the way to the ceiling, and the cubicles had been made 'safe' by wire mesh nailed to the top. The sheets were anything but clean. My father walked back downstairs and said he didn't really want the room after all. The manager looked at him, said, 'I thought you wouldn't,' and gave him back his fifty cents. After this my father walked on until he came to a slightly better hotel, where a room with a private bath cost five dollars. He checked in, then went out to a bar and had a beer and listened to the people talking around him; later he let his bathtub run full to the top and soaked in it while reading a glossy gossip magazine he'd bought.

In the early hours of the morning he woke to the sound of a sleepy, plaintive female voice coming through the wall from the room next door. 'Will you be back?' the voice asked. 'What is your name . . . ?'

I'd like to ask him to tell me more and more, but I don't want to scare him off. I'm afraid of his noticing how greedy I am for a glimpse of who he was before our family existed.

*

This morning something odd happened. My father was still upstairs and I was pottering around in the kitchen when I saw Giorgio through the window, looking for some sign of life. He had his rake on his shoulder and was wearing his working clothes, yellowed tank-top, jeans, and the dusty sun hat which leaves the top of his forehead white when he dresses to go to town. He was about to mow the hay on our field. He's been doing it for years, ever since Gino gave it up; but he obviously felt embarrassed to be doing it right under my father's nose without asking permission. I asked him in and called my father to come downstairs. When he appeared Giorgio seemed genuinely surprised. 'But you're well, you're still on your feet!'

I keep turning his words over and over in my mind. His eyes were actually moist from emotion.

And it occurs to me that there's nothing they haven't seen here, alcoholism is rife in the countryside. I think of Beppe, with whom my father used to gladly share a drop, who was mute by the end, could only wave from his tractor, open-mouthed as if in amazement. Or Gino's cousin Ettore, the painter, with his mad-genius eyes and the copper plate tied over his midsection to cure his liver (he showed it to us, pulling up his shirt), who used to sit roaring with drunken grandiloquence in Gino and Silvana's little kitchen while they receded and said nothing. Or Cipriano, whom I met only yesterday up in the woods, standing there with his hand-beaten scythe, red-nosed and dim-witted like some primitive personification of death. Not to mention the foreigners . . .

*

My father mentions his 'good friend So-and-So, who later won the Nobel prize.' He tells me how once as a student he thought he had discovered a new species of protozoa, how he overcame a thousand bureaucratic hurdles to be allowed to cross from the French into the American occupation zone to look it up in a reference work in Heidelberg; and how he bicycled all that way only to find that it wasn't a new species after all. He tells it with such a light laugh, but I wonder if it was the beginning of what would become a pattern in his life of being just on the verge of 'something big'; and then the disappointment.

Again we are sitting outside until late, listening to the peaceful sounds from the valley. There is no moon and the stars are spectacular. Pointing, my father tells me about different stars, constellations. For a few moments I am a little girl again, admiring him, learning at his feet.

For a while, he says, he had the ambition to photograph 'globular clusters' – two particular ones, M13 and M15 – with his telescope camera. Once he stayed up the entire night, going to bed only at dawn. But when he had the photos printed, the stars had come out as little lines, and he realized there was a systematic error in his telescope, it didn't follow the movement of the sky quite perfectly. After this his interest waned, and when thieves broke into the house the following year and stole part of his equipment, he wasn't all that upset about it. 'In fact I was even secretly a little relieved.'

*

He tells me about the day the Americans arrived in the village where he and his mother and sisters had taken refuge. Rumour had preceded the soldiers that they were searching every house, taking anything of value. The extended family was thrown into a frenzy of preparations characterized by an instinctive, idiot guile. They set about concealing all things of value, stuffing them into mattresses, burying them in the back yard. My father buried his microscope and his camera, wrapped in oilcloth. Then, on a tray, the women assembled objects with which to conciliate the soldiers: a cheap watch, some silver rings, a cigarette case, and so forth. One aunt had prepared a speech consisting of a single English sentence which she practised over and over as they waited: '*We are poor people.*'

When the soldiers came there were three of them. They were young; one of them was black. No one in the village had ever seen a black person before. They took a brief look around and then one of them asked for a glass of water. My father recalls the moment that followed with particular vividness. His cousin held up the tray of offerings to the soldier who had spoken. She looked all twisted from the combination of her fear of being raped and her sly hope of fooling the soldier into taking the trinkets. My father felt implicated against his will in the abject wretchedness of her gesture. 'A glass of water, please,' the man said again. A frozen silence met his request. He had to repeat it a third time before they were convinced that this was really all the soldiers wanted.

Later, they came to rely on the Americans' generosity. An officer had discovered a German military storehouse containing two things in vast quantities: unprocessed chocolate, and wine. Rather than give these things to his own soldiers, he had them distributed to the populace. 'There was nothing to eat, and then suddenly we had this huge cube of chocolate.' My father gestures a square foot. 'The wine, we carried it home in *buckets*.'

Telling these stories seems to make him more cheerful. We look up at the stars and he says that the night before, he had a vision while he was lying in bed that the sky was filled with books, all of them not yet written. For example a book about the Angelinis, about the people he'd passed in the street earlier that day. Who are these people? What are their lives like? 'So many books that could be written,' he tells me.

*

For a while they stayed with one of the 'three beautiful daughters' of one of my grandfather's elder half-sisters. This daughter had married the manager of a paper factory and they were quite well off. The husband loved sports more than anything; he used to say, '*Sport! Sport! − Und ein dunkles Glas Wein*.' The way my father imitates him, he makes the word sound like a vicious, yapping bark: *shpart!* And then, when he had his glass of dark wine, he'd say, philosophically, '*Ja, ja*.' He was eventually found lying dead in a field somewhere. Both he and his wife ended up dying of drink. 'It was a horrible family.' Their eldest son was crippled, he had something wrong with his hip, as a result of which he had to take a lowly job and married beneath his class. My father thinks he and his wife 'went down the same tube,' because when he visited them many years later he was offered a glass of *Schnaps* for breakfast.

It strikes me when I hear such things that there's a ubiquity, a sort of inevitability about drinking, as if it had been a door that had always stood open, a door at the back of my father's mind that had waited patiently, until it became familiar, until it seemed only a matter of time before he went through it.

*

My father attributes my insomnia to a depressive tendency. 'In this too you resemble me,' he comments. His depression, he says, comes on suddenly, 'like a sore throat.'

*

All day long I feel dull-witted or absent-minded; I realize only later that the whole time I was unconsciously trying to gauge my father's state of mind. He has begun to sleep later in the mornings, to take naps in the afternoon. He apologizes for being depressed, for not feeling well, his stomach is off, he needs to lie down. 'I don't want to spoil your mood.' I observe myself at such moments, the shutting down, refusal to feel anything. 'Fine, fine,' I say, and, 'Never mind.' Complete uncertainty as to what it's really about.

'Take stronger medicine,' I actually tell him at one point.

He accuses me of not taking his illness seriously. I maintain a stony silence, incapable of saying what I think.

There has been a slight turn or shift in our interactions, our friendliness with each other is becoming a bit forced.

In the pizzeria: the defiant move with which he snatched away the stool the waitress had put at our table and replaced it with a chair. As if he were used to being treated disrespectfully and had learned to defend himself. I felt glad, proud that he was standing up for himself, yet at the same time sad. Afterwards he went back and gave the waitress a handsome tip.

At lunch I ask him if he remembers his father at all. 'Yes, sure, I think of him quite frequently.' What was he like? 'Easygoing.'

I remember an acquaintance once used the same word, 'easygoing', to describe my father; but in his case, nothing could be further from the truth.

'But I used to get on his nerves,' my father adds. He remembers how once, when he was proudly telling at dinner about the female white *Lasius flavus* ant he had captured, his father exploded – '*Lasius Scheißus!*' – hitting the table with the palm of his hand.

'What's *wrong* with that boy! Why can't he speak *German* for God's sake!' My father says he began using Latin words even more, on purpose, to provoke him.

The war was long over when the family finally learned what had happened to my grandfather. He had never been a Russian prisoner. A lieutenant who had been with him at the end, and had survived, wrote my grandmother a letter upon his own return from Russia, describing how my grandfather had died from a head wound not far from the family's home in Oliva.

'Yes, I do think that I loved my *Papi*,' my father says, as if answering, finally, a question that had been posed many years ago.

*

Again and again we discuss what to do about Collina. The walls of the house are being eroded, with swallows and wasps building their nests in giant holes. The once-new shutters are rotting away, brambles are reclaiming the terrace and engulfing the well; the *stalla* has become a junkyard filled with the rubble of abandoned projects. But at the same time as Collina is falling slowly to pieces, my father is making ever more grandiose plans for it. A complete stucco job; a road deviation that will leave the house in splendid isolation, making it, as the locals have told him, egging him on to spend his money, 'almost like a villa.' *Villa Collina*. My father is mesmerized by the figures for what these projects will cost: eight million, fifteen million, twenty million lire. He repeats them as if dazzled by the prospect of his own total bankruptcy.

One day he will ask my opinion concerning the various improvements he is contemplating; the next he will say that he is thinking of selling Collina, in order to hear me say that I love it too much, that it would break my heart if he gave it away.

*

My father is upstairs, taking a mid-afternoon bath. He calls it his 'feast'. The bathroom window is open and from the terrace I can hear him splashing and whistling *Summertime*. Then the whistling stops. He mutters as he soaps himself. First it is: 'Oh, this is wonderful.' Then something I can't understand, in a different mood: intense, tightly wound, like a voice in an argument. I hold my breath, listening. After another pause, I hear: 'It never ends,' wistfully, in English.

A kind of hollow opens up inside me, a bottomless ache. I can't do anything for him, I can't help him.

*

When we were on sabbatical in California, where I dreaded going to school each day, he used to walk me to the bus stop every morning in the dark, even though I was old enough to have gone by myself. How to tell him I remember these things.

My father tells me that along with anti-depressant medication, his doctor has ordered 'that I treat myself well, do something nice for myself.' So he has bought a new car, a red Alfa Romeo. The doctor in question, as I know, is still his old loyal Dr Uhland. 'Maybe you should find a new doctor,' I suggest coldly.

*

It's late in the morning, I know my father's awake. Why doesn't he come out of his room? His door is closed, but there's a crack through which I can see him, sitting motionless at the small table with his head in his hands. It is a pose of despair. How long has he been sitting this way? Stricken with fear, I pass his door a couple more times, very slowly, on tiptoe. Peering in at my father. Spying on him through the crack in the door.

I wish I could see inside him, see what is going through his mind.

*

He continually mentions that he is close to seventy, how difficult it is for him to leave his life's profession, how depressed he is. He talks about making his will. I think: he is actually casting himself as a dying man, a man on the brink of death. His plea for sympathy provokes in me a desire to be brutal.

And there's a bad edge to his behaviour as well. His talk about wills is an attempt to entrap me. When he asks, 'What do you want?', naming this or that object, trying to lure me into expressing an interest, it's a disguised accusation that I'm after his money.

'I still make the most money of any of you, even though I'm retired.'

I've decided to return my father's next cheque, not to accept money from him ever again.

*

'I wasn't going to tell you this,' my father says, 'but, well, I guess I'm going to tell you anyway.' We're sitting in the pizzeria in Pontecchio and the TV is on, showing a Formula Uno race. Two months ago he was driving to Stuttgart to visit my grandmother, racing along the autobahn in his red Alfa, doing about 160 kilometres per hour. 'Speed makes you high, that's a known fact.' Passing a Peugeot, he veered a little too abruptly back into the right lane. He lost control, the car spun round, seconds later he found himself, dazed and breathless, on the grassy embankment by the side of the highway. The people he had passed stopped and came back to see if he was hurt. But there was nothing wrong with him at all. The Alfa – not a scratch.

On the way back he carefully checked the terrain by the side of the autobahn: there was not a single other place along the entire stretch where he could have landed so unharmed.

In the Formula Uno race we are watching as we eat our pizzas the German driver, Michael Schumacher, moves into the lead. My father puts on a show of nationalistic enthusiasm, chanting loudly, '*Schu-mi! Schu-mi!*' – jumping up and down in his seat, boxing the air. There's provocation in his buffoonery; he does this to embarrass me, knowing how easily I am embarrassed in public. He pours himself a large glass of wine with a defiant gesture: '*Prost!*' A little later there is an accident; you can see the crumpled metal of the car that was in third place, and they appear to be removing a body. My father is silent now. After what seems a long time the race is finally stopped. 'I think the driver must be dead,' my father says.

But it turns out he has only broken his legs.

*

'Countrymen of yours,' my father remarks venomously when we see a group of Americans in the piazza. He makes anti-American comments at every opportunity. I wonder if this has something to do with the gratitude and guilt that were forced on him at the age of sixteen, in addition to his resentment because we have all moved back to America.

He asks me: don't I want to know if he knew about the concentration camps, about what was going on? I look at him blankly. I've always simply assumed he was too young. But he wants me to ask him, it seems he wants to get this off his chest. 'Well, I knew that they existed because once I made some remark and my best friend said to me, "*Sag sowas nicht, sonst kommst du ins Konzertlager.*" Don't say things like that or you'll go to the concert camp. He used that joking term for it. But,' my father says, 'I had no clear idea what they were and I couldn't ask my parents. I honestly can't tell you what they knew. I hope you believe me.'

*

He tells me about the trip he and my mother took to Mexico and Guatemala when I was three, leaving me with my mother's mother in California. Puebla, Oaxaca, Chichicastenango. A bus ride into the jungle when they had 'the trots'. There were few tourists then, some of the Indians had never seen blond people before. (My mother with her blond curls, doing watercolours.) My father remembers a man who approached them in a café because he wanted to practise his English; then invited them to his villa for dinner. There was a heavy, ornate iron gate with an Indian sleeping behind it under a blanket; the Indian was awakened to open the gate for them. At the front door of his house, their host drew a heavy pistol from under his jacket. My parents thought he was going to shoot them, or hold them up, but he only used it to knock on the door, summoning his wife. The evening was spent stiffly in freezing cold, barely furnished rooms.

'And then we used to go, like zombies, from one antique store to another.' They found a sixteenth-century French silver-plated microscope for five dollars, pre-Columbian sculptures. In order to afford them they scrimped on food, stayed in the dingiest hotels. 'We were so thrifty. I was thrifty then, too.' They mailed back their dirty clothes and filled their suitcases with treasures.

My father would like to go back in style, to stay in 'the Grand Hotel in Chichi'.

Again and again my father brings up my mother's 'thrift'. How he once missed an opportunity to buy a priceless antique clock for $50 and instead bought something much smaller for $5. How they got soaked sleeping in tents on their first trip to Italy, when a comfortable hotel would have cost only a little bit more. To my mother, the bad in my father is what he became at the end, whereas he remembers things about her that always bothered him. There is an unfairness in this asymmetry; I feel hurt for my mother.

I wonder how much this has influenced my choices in life: not wanting to be caught in her position.

✳

Screwing up my courage, I've broached the topic of his drinking. He was standing at the top of the stairs, on the way to his room, and I was two-thirds of the way down. Both of us maintaining casual postures and speaking lightly, as if of some unimportant matter, as if it weren't the first time we'd talked about it since we went on that walk together more than fifteen years ago. At first he seemed relieved, even grateful that the matter was out in the open. But now all that has come of it is that he's begun to make little jokes, trivializing it. He says smugly about an acquaintance, a professor of philosophy, 'He is much worse off than I.'

He says he would rather die than have to give up drinking altogether. It comes down to this: drinking has replaced all other reasons for living.

I am wearing down, I'm becoming allergic to my father. He gets on my nerves. It's an involuntary physical reaction: everything about him annoys me. His muttering to himself, the loud belching. The going back and forth, travelling hither and thither. The expression on his face when he stares at me when I'm reading. His continuous talk about making a will, his sighs, the way he pours himself another and another glass of wine. Merely to have to witness the way he lives, in the narrow confinement of his needs, the needs of his broken-down bowels, of his blood for alcohol, his liver for milk products: to have to watch him turning round and around in the small circle formed by these needs, is torture for me.

I have a notion he is constantly at work inventing fabulous forms of freedom for himself, such as his reincarnation as the food critic of *Zeit Magazin*, or the idea that he has willed his own destruction, that he has plunged himself on purpose into failure, out of sheer curiosity or a bold taste for piquancy. I imagine his mind as a sort of termitary, an intricate three-dimensional labyrinth in which he hides from himself.

*

He tells me that Silke went to London a few months back to attend a Christie's auction of 'a Picasso series' from her family's collection. I can tell how impressed he is and how he wants me to be impressed. He describes the luxury cruise he and

Silke took last year, up the coast of Norway to Spitzbergen, almost as far as the North Pole. They came within touching distance of icebergs, saw polar bears, it was so cold that they had to wear half a dozen layers plus life-jackets for the twice or thrice daily excursions to islands in rubber dinghies. But it's the opulent lifestyle on board that seems to have impressed him most. In advance of each meal they were informed of the dress code: casual, formal, or 'festive'. In contrast to his lack of appetite here at Collina, where he is barely able to swallow down his yogurts, on that ship he rose to the occasion. He started breakfast with two slices of smoked salmon, then he ate two thick American-style pancakes with butter in between and maple syrup poured over the top and two slices of smoked bacon on the side.

Now, whenever he brings up the theme of making his will, I have a ready response. Not without an element of cruelty, I tell him that he should use his money up, he should 'enjoy life'. I suggest other adventurous trips he might take, on the Orient Express for example, or the Trans-Siberian Railway. He likes that idea. 'But it would have to be first class.'

It occurs to me that this was part of Silke's attraction for him: that she reminded him of his own family's lost fortune, their lost worldly estate. Silke's casual insouciance about money was something that my father recognized as his lost birthright. Perhaps his enduring hatred of my mother's 'thrift' really is a clue, it's a class thing, he found it demeaning.

My mother who, when they became engaged, paid off the debts he had accumulated with her *chicken money*.

Perhaps I am constitutionally incapable of acknowledging that my father's and Silke's love could have been as real a love as the one that conceived me — as if to recognize this would somehow unravel who I am, or give me a new definition that I am unwilling to accept.

✳

I am increasingly cold and distant. I barely make any effort at conversation any more. I hide behind the pose of the 'observer'. I go into my room and close the door with an air of purposefulness so that he will think I'm 'working'; but I'm not really, I'm just staring out the window.

On one occasion I overreact to something he says, I blow up at him for virtually no reason. He looks at me with incomprehension, with astonishment. 'I didn't mean anything by it,' he says meekly.

✳

At dinner my father suddenly says that he is full and can't finish his plate. I say it doesn't matter and go on eating, but it's almost as if he wanted to make a point of rejecting the food. When I reach for the salad bowl he pushes his own plate toward me. 'Here is some salad, I can't finish it.' Abruptly he says that he wants to go to bed; there's an obstinacy about it, as if he were pushing me away like his plate, as if he wanted to dismiss the world with a wave of his hand.

His withdrawal is a withdrawal from me.

He has never even mentioned receiving the letter I wrote to him, but now I realize it's been at the back of his mind all along. Of course he read the rejection in it clearly. Of course he sees me with complete clarity. He knows that I'm counting the days here with him, knows that in all our conversations I've managed to tell him nothing of myself.

✳

Once again I am sleepless. The irregular slanting rafters of the roof stretch out over me; I used to think of them as the ribs of a huge protective wing. I am tired when I go to bed, but then the thought of lying like a dead person under a blanket on one side of the hallway while my father lies sleeping on the other is so repugnant to me that I am wide awake again. Even though both our doors are closed I imagine that the sound of his breathing has followed me, I can still hear it, that slight under-the-breath whistling interrupted by the occasional silent hiccup or muttering. I am filled with enormous hostile restlessness. I fantasize confrontations with him, everything spilling out. At moments like this I wouldn't be sorry never to see Collina again.

I manage to interpret even his complete powerlessness as a perverse threat of power over me.

*

At five in the morning a wave of despair hits me at the thought of facing another day with him.

*

My father continually says '*Ich HASSE*' this and that; sometimes, when I hear him through a closed door, I can only hear this part of the sentence: 'I HATE . . .' but not what it is that he hates. After the clear and loud emphasis of *hasse* the rest is mumbled. It could be anything, any small, trivial thing, like getting up early, 'the breakfast roll waiting for me on my plate.' The object is dwarfed, squashed, literally overwhelmed by the emotion. When he said to me, '*Ich liebe dich*,' I had the feeling he was expressing a momentary release from his hatred even of me; the way he could say one day, '*Ich liebe Collina*,' and the next that he hated it. Those moments when he could say '*Ich liebe*,' there seemed to be a feeling of tremendous relief, as if, after being shut for a long time in a dark, airless room, he had suddenly been given a ray of light and a breath of fresh air.

＊

My father is retching over the bathroom sink. I can barely force myself to ask, 'Are you not well?' My voice is devoid of compassion. I am overwhelmed by an anger so strong it's as if I'd been turned to stone. 'Yes indeed I am not well,' he replies savagely. Later, going back to his room, he apologizes pathetically: 'I'm sorry, I didn't mean it,' and closes the door.

＊

His physical repulsiveness, the skin of his face that's wrinkled and leathery; the enormous paunch. The horrible 'artistic' shirt, that my brother says looks 'like Hawaii off-season'.

We call off our plan to visit neighbours, my father doesn't feel up to it. I suggest a little drive in the car instead. 'I think I would throw up.' He says what he has is 'Collina-itis'.

'Everybody's *urging* me to *go* somewhere, to *do* something!'

＊

My father sitting on the terrace at Collina, by himself, sitting at his dinner table overlooking the landscape, the sunset, like a solitary king surveying his realm, eating gorgonzola out of the paper and blackberry jam out of the jar. On the chequered cloth there stands a bottle of Chianti and at the two opposite corners of the table he has placed dishes of blackberry jam which are for the wasps, his table companions.

'Here, that is for you,' he is saying. His voice rumbles. 'Here's something for your dinner. – No, *this* is *mine*, *that* is *yours*.'

He is talking to the wasps. They are his friends. I am not his friend. He barely acknowledges me as I approach. He is angry at me because I've gone away, he believes I have abandoned him.

And then the killing spree: at a certain point they get to be too much for him and he begins swatting every wasp that comes his way. He keeps count, collects his victims in a jar: by the end of the massacre he has killed forty-seven wasps.

*

It is the middle of my last day in Collina and my father is lying in bed, curled up under two blankets. 'I'm fine, I'm fine,' he says. 'I was just a little tired. I'll get up soon.'

Then, toward evening, there he is, half-kneeling on the floor in the dining room with the telephone receiver at his ear.

'*Hallo? Mutti?*' He is making a long-distance call to my grandmother in Stuttgart.

It reminds me of something he told me a few days ago about his childhood in Danzig. Because his room was too far away from his mother's for her to be able to hear him if he called, there was a button installed near his bed that activated an electric bell in her room. He remembers pushing the button often, summoning her in the night for the slightest of reasons, because he'd heard a noise, or wanted a glass of water. Sometimes he called her for nothing. He'd say, 'Now I've forgotten what I wanted.'

They called that bell *die Nachtglocke*, the night bell.

He's calling his mother now just to say that everything is all right, yes, yes, everything is all right with him.

'And – Mutti? I just wanted to say, I love you.'

I can't believe what I'm hearing. For a moment I wouldn't be surprised to see the phone cord dangling loose, disconnected:

my father's words don't seem to go anywhere but remain block-ishly, preposterously, in the room. I realize at once that the message, too late to reach my grandmother, is really intended for me. It's for my benefit that he's putting on this act. It's a reproach, his way of telling me that this is what he wants from me.

My father tries to pry the words out of me, to extort them from me, but I resist him. It's like some fairy tale I vaguely remember or imagine, in which something golden must not see the light of day, or be named, lest it turn to dirt. I feel that if I were to say to my father, 'I love you,' the words would become a lie, and he would never again be able to believe or even hope that this is true.

*

My father told me a dream he had: he and I got lost on the road up to Collina. We walked and walked but we couldn't find the house and we ended up in a totally different, strange place.

29

I am sitting at Gilli's, the large, old, elegant café in Piazza della Repubblica; since Daniel and I have been in Florence I've been coming here for coffee a couple of times a week. When my waiter sees me he merely asks 'The usual?' At this moment the place is beautiful, with the morning sunlight streaming in onto the blond wood, onto the faded pink walls and the yellow silk tablecloths covered with white lace. There is a sparrow that lives inside here; it just flew down from some high place to the floor and is hopping about, marvelled at by the guests, momentarily creating a link between us of exchanged smiles and questioning glances. Across the room sits the scholar whom I've seen before, who seems also to be a regular. I call him a scholar now even though the first time I saw him I thought he was a priest in civilian clothes, reading through his sermon. Today, too, he's going over some kind of typescript; he has grey hair and he keeps readjusting the distance of his reading glasses from his eyes, pushing them now closer, now farther away, as if obsessed with the idea that he can't see properly.

The glasses are attached to a cord that goes around his neck; it makes a black line traversing his cheek.

Everything here, now, every detail of light and shadow and the way the waiter's face changes as he walks out of the shadow into the light, seems precious and interesting. There is more than I can grasp all at once and I feel a great urgency to write everything down.

There are two petite strawberry-blonde French ladies who look nice for their age and are identical twins; they've come on vacation with their husbands who look like brutes. One of these brutes keeps looking at the woman who is not his wife, perhaps he's fallen in love with his sister-in-law who looks just like his wife but for the hairstyle and the fact that she seems happier and has fewer worry-creases than his wife. For my part, in the course of watching them I've come to think of the two women as vastly different, while their husbands seem to me nearly identical.

Last night when we went out for dinner Daniel caught me staring at some people again; I am so interested in people I don't know that it seems I go into a kind of trance, I lose all awareness of myself, of him, of the conversation we were just having. Suddenly I am completely absorbed in a little family sitting near us, an American couple and their young son. I'm not consciously thinking about them but am just intent on not missing the slightest flicker that passes over their faces as they interact with each other. It's terribly rude but Daniel knows me, he just touches my arm to bring me back. Then he imitates comically the face that I make, my fixed expression as I peer out the corners of my eyes.

It is Daniel's research that has given us this year of vaga-bondage; he is working on a fourteenth-century mercenary captain who left traces of his activity all over Italy. Sometimes we go to cafés together, I with my coloured notebooks, he with his scads of paper, his chronicles, his illegible archival notes. We sit at different tables, spreading ourselves out; once in a while we'll look up as if seeing each other for the first time.

The first time my father met Daniel, before we were married, he said to me afterwards, 'He is a bit like me.' It was clear to me from the pondering, thoughtful way he said it that he knew perfectly well it was untrue. Daniel neither resembles my father nor is he his opposite: he is completely different, unrelated. He is a new world.

*   *   *

For a little while, after we had said goodbye and I had left my father in Collina, I had a feeling as if it were all so simple. It was too late to fear or hope for anything, too late to do anything about it any more. I couldn't help him and I couldn't run away. Neither of us could change anything. There was, perhaps on both sides, a sense of resignation that was liberating.

My aunt Hannelore recently told me, as if rehearsing a familiar fact, that my father as a young boy was shy and did not have many friends. For some reason, when she said this it struck me as a revelation. Something about the assurance with which she invoked the cliché of the 'lonely child': the complete discrepancy between her plaintively sad idea and my own memory of childhood, in which loneliness wasn't sad at all but was as elemental and neutral as milk. Up until that moment I had always thought the question was, Am I like him? Family resemblance meant a passing down, the threat of repetition. The revelation was: 'He is like me.' It was as though, through a simple shift in perception, time could be made irrelevant. Not that the clock could be turned back: but I could imagine in reverse. I could imagine the present as a beginning with respect to the past, or me as a beginning with respect to him. I could conceive my father out of myself. All of this came to me in a single vague flash, an idea remote from words, but infinitely consoling. It seemed like the solution to some problem that had been troubling me for a long time.

Perhaps it's something I am learning, a feeling that will come back more and more often. These days I find myself wanting to call my father on the phone, not to say anything in particular, but just to keep in touch, to see how he is doing. He tells me now that he wants to take up photography again. He is going to use Silke's laundry room in the basement as a darkroom. He has already assembled much of the apparatus he needs: enlarger, infra-red lights, plastic pans for the baths. He says he has a couple of rolls of film that he's never developed; he's anxious to see what's on them.

Another time he mentions that he has a doctor's appointment. After we've chatted for a few minutes about other things he comes out and tells me the doctor he's seeing is across the border in Switzerland, 'He's a psychiatrist, but really more like a friend, we just talk, he asks me questions and encourages me, tells me how many things I still have to look forward to.'

*

I am visiting Vienna and some strange compulsion makes me go to the Museum of Natural History. I am almost alone in this immense building; no one comes here, while crowds throng up the stairs to the Art Museum, facing it. Even before entering, I know exactly what I want to see: the insects. I pass quickly by the nematodes, the shellfish. When I come to the great hall of insects, large enough to be a concert hall, with case upon case ranged in parallel rows, containing hundreds of thousands of specimens, I know instantly that it's everything I wanted. I stay for hours, strolling slowly past the displays. And I'm not sure whether I've come for the insects themselves, for the gradual modulations and almost imperceptible variations, harmless plant-eaters side by side with murderous parasites, for their unbelievable iridescences (but it's not beauty I'm after); or whether it isn't rather the minute spindly labels that have drawn me here, the oldest hand-lettered in ink that has faded to brown. The labels are strangely moving, they seem like the ghosts of generations of daredevil collectors and patient classifiers, heroic in the face of nature's mindless, infinite invention.

Afterwards I call my father and tell him casually that I've been to the Natural History Museum. I specify: I've seen the insects. He says, excitedly, 'But I was there too, years ago. I don't know, has it been thirty, forty years? I remember that, yes, I *remember* that! There were creatures so microscopic, they were smaller than the diameter of a pin and they'd still managed to mount them . . . That's unbelievable, you went there too!'

As my father tells me this I suddenly feel as though subconsciously I'd known it all along: as though I'd really gone to this unpopular, silent, forsaken place with the secret hope of meeting him there.

ACKNOWLEDGEMENTS

I wish to thank Julian Anderson, James Gordon Bennett, Beth Clary, Bette Howland, Jacob and Jennifer Howland, and Suzanne Thomson, for their encouragement and helpful comments on early drafts of this manuscript. I am also deeply grateful to my agent, Sam Boyce, and to my editors, Victoria Hutchinson and Mary Mount, for their faith and hard work in bringing the book to completion. And I owe special thanks to Colm Tóibín, without whom it might never have seen the light of day.

I would like to thank Derek Weiler, my brother and literary guide, for many readings and crucial advice, and for having introduced me to my favorite books.

Most of all, I would like to thank my husband, Bill Caferro, who gives me the courage to write. He has read the manuscript at every stage; his critical judgment and good humour have helped me more than I can say.